Robert Bridges

Overheard in Arcady

Robert Bridges

Overheard in Arcady

ISBN/EAN: 9783743303751

Manufactured in Europe, USA, Canada, Australia, Japa

Cover: Foto ©Andreas Hilbeck / pixelio.de

Manufactured and distributed by brebook publishing software
(www.brebook.com)

Robert Bridges

Overheard in Arcady

OVERHEARD IN ARCADY

BY

ROBERT BRIDGES

ILLUSTRATED BY OLIVER HERFORD,
F. G. ATTWOOD, AND A. E. STERNER

NEW YORK
CHARLES SCRIBNER'S SONS
1894

To My Mother

Long years you've kept the door ajar
To greet me, coming from afar;
Long years in my accustomed place
I've read my welcome in your face,
And felt the sunlight of your love
Drive back the years and gently move
The tell-tale shadow 'round to youth.
You've found the very spring, in truth,
That baffles time—the kindling joy
That keeps me in your heart a boy.
And now I send an unknown guest
To bide with you and snugly rest
Beside the old home's inglenook.—
For love of me you'll love my book.

CONTENTS

*** The author begs to acknowledge the kindness of J. A. Mitchell, editor of *Life*, in permitting him to use the original illustrations with these articles which were published in *Life* over the signature *Droch*.

W. D. HOWELLS

THE HOUSEHOLD OF W. D. HOWELLS

BROMFIELD CORRY, ESQ., . . . A Boston Gentleman.
BARTLEY HUBBARD, ... Reporter of the Boston *Events*.
FULKERSON, ... { Business Manager of the New
                              { York *Every Other Week*.
MISS ANNIE KILBURN, ... A New England Old Maid.
MISS PENELOPE LAPHAM, . . { Daughter of Silas Lapham, and
                            { betrothed to Tom Corey.

SCENE: *A Parlor Car on the Express train from Boston to
New York.*

HUBBARD (*rushing in late, and recognizing* FUL-
KERSON *as he subsides*): Hello, Fulkerson! What
have you been doing in Boston? No one in a real
literary centre like ours ever heard of *Every Other
Week*.

FULKERSON: That's why I came over. I've been
to see all your Boston publishers and struck them for
Ads. I simply said: "Gentlemen, Boston is the intellectual hub of the United States—no doubt of it.
New York is on the outer rim of the whirlpool of
Thought. In your town everybody writes books, nobody reads them; in New York everybody reads them,
nobody has a mind to write them. Hence, the wise

3

publisher makes his books in Boston and sells them in New York. A page advertisement in New York will bring you ten orders to one from the same space in Boston. *Moral*—advertise in *Every Other Week* at $100 a page and save $900. See!'' And they saw me for $2,000 worth of contracts in my left-hand pocket.

HUBBARD: Whew! That's better than writing interviews; guess I'll turn business manager; but I'll go on to New York first and interview Howells. I owe him a few.

FULKERSON (*laughing*): He *did* you up brown in "A Modern Instance"—made a sort of Terrible Example of you. Still, you oughtn't to kick. I hear the *Events* raised your space-rate on the strength of your notoriety, and that scores of Solid Men of Boston offered you bribes to put them in your series of interviews.

HUBBARD (*with satisfaction*): Oh, yes. I've even been asked to contribute a weekly budget of Boston scandal to a New York paper, and call it "Society News." I'm right in the swim now, my boy.

FULKERSON (*looking toward* COREY, *who has just returned* HUBBARD's *nod in a freezing manner*): Who is your friend who is not quite sure that he ought to recognize you in public?

HUBBARD: Oh, that is Bromfield Corey, Esq., a

real Boston Brahmin. I tried to interview him once on the rumored engagement of his son, Tom Corey, to old Silas Lapham's daughter Penelope, and he snubbed me cold. (*With surprise.*) By Jove! there she is in the seat in front of him, and he does not seem to know her from Eve—different layer of society, you know! I might score a point now by introducing him to his future daughter-in-law as though we were old acquaintances. I met her once at a Veterans' ball in which Colonel Lapham was interested. Here goes! (*Rising.*) Mr. Corey, you ought to know Miss Penelope Lapham, who is sitting near you. This is Mr. Bromfield Corey, Miss Lapham. You've possibly heard of him from his son. I've met you both professionally, you know; reporter of the *Events;* going to New York to interview Howells; want to know why he has left Boston for New York—what he thinks of the Four Hundred as intellectual material—why he has put my friend Fulkerson, here, in a novel—and all that sort of thing. But you don't know Fulkerson? Business Manager of *Every Other Week*—chained lightning in booming his sheet—full of schemes and bound to win. Look around, Fulkerson! Here are some Boston people who have heard of your paper and want to know you. Miss Lapham, this is Mr. Fulkerson; Mr. Corey, you must know my friend. Curious, isn't it, that Howells should have put us all in his books? And there is another of us! Miss Annie Kilburn, of Hatboro'; met her when I went down

5

there to write up the Northwick defalcation. Miss Kilburn, I want to introduce a lot of friends of Mr. Howells to you—all met by chance in a parlor-car. (*Presents everybody.*) Now I have an idea. While we are waiting for the call to dinner, let us give our opinions of Howells. He has given the world his opinion of us ; let us return the compliment. I give you my word, Mr. Corey, I shan't publish it—just a little " literary symposium " to pass away the time. See ! Come, Miss Lapham, youth and beauty first, you know !

PENELOPE (*looking shyly at* COREY) : Oh, I can't say exactly what I think about Mr. Howells ! He helped me once out of a great trouble. I wanted to make a life-long sacrifice to what I thought was Duty. It would have made several people miserable for life, but I thought that did not matter so long as it was Duty. Then he showed me that what many people called Duty was an extreme form of selfishness which liked to pride itself on its monopoly of suffering. (*Blushing at her own earnestness.*) I can't speak calmly about it, for it has brought me such happiness to see things in the natural light he has put them in.

MISS KILBURN (*aside to* PENELOPE) : Dear child, he has helped older people than you to be happy when they really wanted to be miserable.

COREY (*looking distrustfully at* HUBBARD) : Of course one does not like to talk publicly about one's best friends ; but I have read Howells a long time,

6

and I have gone through several changes of opinion about him.

MISS KILBURN : I can guess how you felt. Long ago you read " The Undiscovered Country," and you thought that the legitimate successor of Hawthorne had arrived ?

COREY (*smiling*) : No ; not quite that. That is the feminine version of it. A man past middle life does not look for the " successor " to anybody. This whole show of living and working loses continuity. At forty, this is a World of Chance ; at sixty, we begin to believe in Providence again ; and at eighty, I hope to be as a little child and say *Adsum* with Colonel Newcome.

MISS KILBURN : You are wandering away from " The Undiscovered Country." What *did* you think then ?

COREY : Well, fifteen years ago I thought many things that I should not dream of now. For one, I thought Howells was a romantic novelist.

MISS KILBURN : Perhaps he *was* then. I don't believe that the change is all in us.

COREY : I am always a good decade ahead of him in age ; and when I read him I have a vivid impression of looking back on my own experiences and observations. I suspect that he has always written with the utmost fidelity the impressions that the world has made on him. In youth, they were romantic, as they are in all healthy organisms ; in early maturity, they had a little of that cruelty of realism which

7

comes to every man when he first ceases to find his own sensations the chief thing in life, and looks at other people ; and now in middle life, in the light of experience, he sees more than ever the inherent pathos in living. That is why the social problem seems to be the supreme thing to him now.

FULKERSON (*cutting in*) :   He's on the right tack. As a man of business I can vouch for that.   What the great public wants to read about is its own misery, with directions for hypnotizing it into happiness. That is why " Looking Backward " sold ; and I am told that " A Hazard of New Fortunes " is the most popular of Howells's books, for the same reason.

HUBBARD :   No, no, my boy.   You are too modest.   That book sold because *you* are in it.   The average American likes to read about a howling business success, and you filled the bill.

COREY (*ironically to* ANNIE KILBURN) :   I have often wondered why Mr. Howells devoted so much time and space to unimportant people.   One does not care to meet them, and I don't see why one should care to read about them.

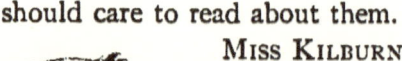

MISS KILBURN :   Aren't they a big part of the big world, Mr. Corey ?   Perhaps it is just a phase of Mr. Howells's scheme to hold the mirror up to reality.

COREY (*meditatively*) : Perhaps.   But one has such

a wide choice of realities in this world, that one may like to spend most of one's time with realities which are of importance.

MISS KILBURN :   Yes ; if you happen to be born in that environment.   Now, I confess that I tried living with " important people " in Europe for several years, and then returned to the commonplaces of Hatboro' with positive relief.   It seems to me that I get an insight of finer shades of life in that provincial atmosphere.

COREY (*philosophically*) :   You've caught the " tail-feather of a great truth," Miss Kilburn.   The finest things in life are matters of the affections, and somehow you only thoroughly comprehend them in the particular environment where you have spent your youth.   That is why " Adam Bede " and " David Copperfield " are the truest novels of their authors.

FULKERSON (*who has been talking with* PENELOPE *and* HUBBARD) :   Oh, I say, what are you so serious about over there ?   We've been pulling Howells to pieces, and Hubbard says he'll try to work us in his interview, after all, as a sort of chorus.   Miss Lapham says that most of the girls she knows are down on Howells's novels because the love-making is so matter-of-fact.

HUBBARD :   Isn't it always matter-of-fact to everybody except the victims ?

MISS LAPHAM :   Well, when we read a novel don't we want the victim's point of view ?

COREY :   You must not take your novels so seriously, my dear. The woman who takes her fiction seriously is apt to take life frivolously. Take them half-and-half.

HUBBARD (*cutting in*) : Howells's views of love and socialism don't interest me a bit ; but I want to give him a straight tip on his idea of journalism. He doesn't seem to realize that it is a great profession which owes a big duty to the public ; and that, just as lawyers, doctors, and preachers have to do things which are very unpleasant to some of the parties concerned, so the reporter must, in the line of duty, do the disagreeable occasionally. *I've* had to, myself.

COREY (*with intention*) : I don't doubt it.

HUBBARD : My theory is that the newspaper is just as important in keeping the world straight as the old belief in future punishment was. Most people have lost all fear of Hades, but they are sure, at any rate, that the press will find them out. I tell you, sir (*looking at* COREY), that a healthy conscience isn't a circumstance to a good, live newspaper in restraining evil in a community.

COREY : It does fight the devil with fire.

HUBBARD : Why, sir, it keeps the American newspaper-man busy running down the wickedness that has been inspired by the American novel. I never wrote up a big crime that I did not find the suggestion of it in a novel hidden somewhere among the criminal's baggage. Fact !

FULKERSON : I haven't any doubt that if Hubbard were given his dues as a great moral force he would

10

be either the president of a City Re-
form Club or a bishop.

HUBBARD: A bishop is a good
enough job for me.

WAITER (*passing through the car*):
Dinner is ready in the dining-car.
First call to dinner! (*All rise to go
to dinner.*)

MISS KILBURN (*to* PENELOPE, *who
is standing by her*): Those men don't
like Mr. Howells because he sees through
the pretences with which they bolster up their vanity.
I suspect that even Mr. Corey is irritated at Howells's
moral earnestness. In Mr. Corey's world manners,
not morals, are the real thing.

HENRY JAMES

THE HOUSEHOLD OF HENRY JAMES

THE MASTER, ...	Henry St. George, novelist.
PAUL OVERT, ...	A young writer.
MISS FANCOURT, ...	A worshipper of genius.
DAISY MILLER, ...	{ A young American from { Schenectady, N. Y.

SCENE: *The library and work-room of* ST. GEORGE, *in the rear of his London house. " A large high room, without windows, but with a wide skylight at the top, like a place of exhibition." The walls covered with book-shelves and prints ; a table littered with proofs and manuscripts ; a large leather lounge, on which* OVERT *is seated smoking.* ST. GEORGE *is pacing back and forth on a strip of brilliant red carpet, the length of the polished floor.*

THE MASTER: It is good of you to leave the ladies upstairs to drink their tea alone, and to come down to this book-factory. I had just reached the end of a paragraph and wanted a smoke.

OVERT (*earnestly*) : It is a great privilege for me to be allowed to interrupt you.

THE MASTER : No, no, my boy ! A talk with you is like a visit from one's old ideals. You see the visions that I saw thirty years ago.

15

OVERT: I hope mine may reach as fine a maturity.

THE MASTER (*looking in his eyes*): You may say polite things upstairs in the drawing-room, but down here we talk to each other's hearts, honestly.

OVERT (*flushing*): You know I admire your achievements——

THE MASTER (*interrupting*): We talked that out once before, and Henry James put it all in his story, "The Lesson of the Master." What a wonderfully subtile man he is! You remember how unconcernedly he sat over there by the hearthstone while we talked, smoking and dreaming as we thought, but all the time seeing through our words into our very hearts. *There* is a man who has followed his Art as I would have you follow it. Don't waste your admiration on this Mess of Pottage which you call my success—this forty volumes, and fine house, and carriages, and titled friends! My boy, my boy, you know better.

OVERT (*critically between rings of smoke*): Yes, I know what you mean. I do admire the way James does it. It is so very well-bred, so even in finish, so delicate in *nuances*. (*Smiling.*) Indeed it is all the other adjectives which artists use in a studio when they are talking about technic. You know the vocabulary! Well, *that* is Henry James—technic, technic, to the end of the story. But I want something more—I want life, with its imperfections, its unreasonableness, its lack of those subtilties which Art spends itself upon.

16

"A TALK WITH YOU IS LIKE A VISIT FROM ONE'S OLD IDEALS."

THE MASTER (*impatiently*) : Please don't go over
all those pet phrases of the hot-blooded young man
who wants to indulge his senses and calls it " study-
ing life." I know them as well as I do the studio
cant about technic. I did not say that you could
learn *everything* from James. But you can learn from
him the possibilities of the English language in sep-
arating emotions which are classed together by the
untrained observer. Surely you have been astounded
at the flexibility of his phrases ? Haven't you learned
from them that our language is delicate, and refined,
as well as virile ?

OVERT : I have, I have ! I read him always with
sensations akin to those with which I watch my own
warm breath turn to wonderfully delicate traceries
of frost on a window-pane. I follow intently the
needle-points of the crystals as they shoot across the
smooth glass, until the apparently hap-hazard lace-
work takes a definite pattern—as though it had been
prearranged from all eternity. Is the breath of life
but a vapor to hang for a few moments in crystals of
frost, and then melt into nothingness ? I rouse from
my reverie chilled to my heart. And *that* is reading
Henry James !

THE MASTER : Your fancy does full credit to your
feeling. What you do not see *now* is that your sensations are the usual chill which Youth feels in con-
tact with Experience. Ten years from now you will
begin to feel the surprising pathos, the warm-blooded
charity, the tolerance of human eccentricity behind

19

this crystal art which chills you. Then you will read " The Liar," " The Middle Years," " The Pupil," with tears in your eyes.

OVERT (*puzzled*): But what has he been driving at all these years that he has worked so faithfully at his art? That is what bothers me. Is he simply doing it for the sake of working?

THE MASTER: He put it all in a phrase once which means more the longer you ponder it. The thing which interests him supremely, which he makes it his mission to depict with his facile art, is *the immitigability of our moral predicament.*

OVERT (*cynically*): The phrase is a polysyllabic terror.

THE MASTER (*smiling*): But, as our American friend drinking tea upstairs would say, " It gets there every time." The tragedy of living is in it—what the philosophers call heredity, environment, predestination and all the other abstractions—but which you and I know as the never-ending daily tussle with those things in us which we would give our very lives to make different. James sees it all as clearly, as pathetically, as any fiction-writer of his generation. We wonder now why his contemporaries called Thackeray a cynic; I suspect that our grandsons will wonder still more why we have called James cold and unsympathetic.

OVERT (*listening to footsteps on the stairs*): There come the young women! Now we shall have new light on the subject.

VOICES (*calling*): Please, may we come down?

THE MASTER: If you don't mind solid chunks of smoke.

OVERT: And a hot discussion.

(*Enter* MISS FANCOURT *and* DAISY MILLER, *in afternoon costume.*)

MISS FANCOURT (*to* OVERT): You promised to go with us to drink tea with the Princess Casamassima.

DAISY MILLER: And meet a lot of artistic and social freaks.

MISS FANCOURT: Henry James will be there, and you always enjoy his talk.

OVERT: Oh, yes, his *talk* is always good.

THE MASTER (*explaining*): James has been the cause of our dispute. Overt thinks he is a cold and unsympathetic artist (*slyly*), and all the other things that the Philistines call him.

MISS FANCOURT (*gushingly*): How can you, Mr. Overt? You, with the soul of an artist under your hat!

DAISY MILLER (*impertinently*): I suspect that his artist-soul is just as conventionally English as his plug hat.

"HOW CAN YOU, MR. OVERT?"

21

"HIS TROLLEY'S OFF THE AMERICAN WIRE."

MISS FANCOURT (*mystified*): What kind of hat?

DAISY MILLER (*laughing*): His plug, dicer, beaver, tile—don't you know your mother tongue?

OVERT: James is an American, but he does not speak your language.

DAISY MILLER (*positively*): And that's what's the matter with Mr. James. If he wrote his native language we'd read him more over the pond.

THE MASTER: I've often wondered why you Americans do not more appreciate him.

DAISY MILLER: Well, I'll tell you. He's lived with you so long that we're not onto his curves. Do you catch on? His trolley's off the American wire. (*The others look at her and at each other in mute astonishment.*) Oh, but you *are* slow at learning the lingo. We used to have a reading club in Schenectady—the girls of our set—to improve our minds, you know. Well, when we had finished " Barriers Burned Away," " St. Elmo," Farrar's " Life of Christ," and " Molly Bawn," one of the girls, a regular blue-stocking from Boston with glasses on her nose, proposed that we read Henry James. That roused my dander. " See here, girls," I said, " if you want to turn this

22

into a circle of King's Daughters to read religious books and sew for the heathen, I'll resign at once." The Boston girl looked shocked and said, "How can you be so rude. Mr. James writes the purest Boston English, and is highly approved by Charles Eliot Norton and the Harvard seniors." (*Sighing.*) Oh, she made me tired. "Why doesn't he come to America again and learn something besides Bostonese!" I said. "We don't all talk like prigs or vulgarians over here! In New York we're refined from our bangs to our boots, and don't you forget it!"

THE MASTER (*getting control of his face*): Thank you. I never understood why James was unpopular in America till I met you.

DAISY MILLER (*protesting*): Oh, you must not take me for a fair sample of an American girl. I had to go abroad for my health before I had had a year at a finishing school in New York. They put a polish on you there in which you can see to comb your hair. Mr. James has not caught on to the fact that we're getting mighty civilized in the States.

THE MASTER (*turning to* MISS FANCOURT): Come, give us an English girl's defence of him.

MISS FANCOURT (*with enthusiasm*): He satisfies my longing for perfection in work. There is never anything in his stories to jar my taste. When he treats a disagreeable subject, he does it as a gentleman would talk about it to a refined woman—with polite phrases, delicate metaphor, and a humor that plays about it all gently. There is none of the heat or prejudice about

23

his stories which is so often evident in the writings of people you would not care to know. When I have finished one of Mr. James's stories I always feel that I should like to meet him in the alcove of a library and talk about it all with him as though it were true. (*Starting.*) And that's what I hope to do at Princess Casamassima's. I want to ask him whether he did not mean "The Real Thing" to be a satire on the artist's point-of-view, as much as on the poor dear gentleman and gentlewoman who tried to be useful. (*To* DAISY *and* OVERT.) Come, the afternoon is almost over !

(*They follow her through the portières after adieus to* THE MASTER.)

THE MASTER (*soliloquizing as he turns to his desk*) : Ah, if I could only clothe my characters with garments woven with James's art they would live for a century or two. But I have marketed my crude inventions for the luxuries of a London establishment, for the pleasures of an ever-present success. But I know, and Overt and James know in their hearts, that it isn't the Real Thing. (*Taking up his pen.*) Come, charlatan, pick up your fool's wand and finish your daily tricks !

THOMAS BAILEY ALDRICH

THE HOUSEHOLD OF
THOMAS BAILEY ALDRICH

MARJORIE DAW, . . . { Only daughter of an old New Eng-
                      { land family.
JOHN FLEMMING, . . . Of New York, rich, and twenty-four.
THE BAD BOY, ... Tom Bailey.

SCENE: *The broad piazza of an old colonial mansion, with gam-*
brel roof and rambling extensions, at the cross-roads near Rye,
N. H. In a shady corner a hammock is swung, and in it a girl
of eighteen, with golden hair and dark eyes, swaying " like a
pond-lily in the golden afternoon." In a wicker chair, very
near the hammock, is JOHN FLEMMING.

MARJORIE DAW (*indignantly*): To think that
Mr. Aldrich *dared* to put it in the story that
there wasn't any colonial mansion, any piazza, any
Marjorie Daw !

JOHN FLEMMING : I believe that he was in league
with Delaney (who must have been in love with you
himself) to throw me off the track and make me give
up the search for the ideal woman I loved.

MARJORIE (*confidently*): He don't know how
steadfast you are.

JOHN (*trying to appear modest*): It was not that
exactly. You see I knew prosaic old Delaney too

27

well to believe that he could invent a girl like you out of whole cloth. I was sure that he had an original in his mind's eye, so I took rooms at the Surf House, and drove all the roads and by-ways 'round Rye till I found you.

MARJORIE (*with beaming face*): And *this* is better than Mr. Aldrich's story?

JOHN (*flattering*): He did not half do you justice. (*The hammock swings conveniently near.*)

MARJORIE: But I like Mr. Aldrich and his stories very much, John, and you must, too. He often comes down this way to Stillwater to call on the Shackfords. You know he wrote a book about them and that awful murder case?

JOHN (*recollecting*): Oh, yes! "The Stillwater Tragedy." Read it when I was laid up with my lame leg; knew Durgin would be the real villain before he had spoken ten words. That is no kind of a detective story. If you want the real thing you ought to read "The Leavenworth Case."

MARJORIE (*severely*): You New York men are such Philistines! Mr. Aldrich is a real man of letters. He would not stoop to detective stories. He writes *literature.*

JOHN (*hedging*): I don't doubt it. But it took something more than mere literature to make me forget that my leg was aching.

MARJORIE (*with a tremble in her voice*): John, if we are to be happy together you must never, never speak lightly of my New England idols.

JOHN (*meekly*):   All right, my dear, make a list of them and I'll worship the whole lot—Emerson, Longfellow, Hawthorne, Lowell, Whittier, Holmes, Aldrich——

MARJORIE (*cutting in*):   Stop, stop!   Don't mention anybody else in the same breath!

JOHN (*curtly*):   Amen!

(*A five minutes' indignant silence, and an affectionate reconciliation.*)

MARJORIE (*in her instructive manner*) : If you are really and truly sorry, you must learn to appreciate Aldrich fully, as I do.

JOHN (*resignedly*) : Go ahead, please ! I'm in a repentant mood.

MARJORIE (*laying down the law*) : You must understand, first, that New England women have a great admiration for Aldrich's work, because so much of it deals with New England people and scenery.

JOHN (*who has been allowed to smoke*) : Queer, isn't it ? You are never tired reading and writing about yourselves. Now in New York most of the men and women I know would rather read anything else than a New York novel.

MARJORIE (*petulantly*) : There are so few of them worth reading.

JOHN (*rising to the occasion on rings of smoke*) : I am not so sure of that. There are Bunner, Janvier, Davis, Hibbard, Bangs, Matthews, Hopkinson Smith, Mrs. Harrison, and Mrs. Cruger—each of them has written a good story or two about New York. But we don't make so much ado about that sort of thing as you do. We have a host of other things to interest us.

MARJORIE : Oh, I know all that. You are rank materialists, and are never worth much till you marry New England girls. (*Coquettishly.*) It isn't a bad combination.

JOHN (*with fervor*) : You bet it isn't !

MARJORIE (*confidently*) : What fun I'll have spiritualizing you! I'll begin with the Aldrich cure. First of all you must read "The Queen of Sheba." It's a love story, and perhaps you are in the mood to appreciate it. Such a charming story, too!

JOHN (*who knows a great deal more than he exhibits*): Let me see? (*Puff, puff.*) Oh, yes, I remember that—girl escapes from a lunatic asylum, meets the hero in a country lane and claims him for her own. Interval; scene shifted to Switzerland— same man, same girl, minus the lunacy; love with intensity, but man made miserable by apprehension of a return of the aforesaid madness. Slow fever— deathbed scene except the *coup de grace;* miraculous recovery. Family physician guarantees a perfect cure of the lunacy. Wedding bells. Curtain. (*Puff, puff.*) Sweet, isn't it?

MARJORIE (*ready to shed tears*): You are a provoking old cynic, and you must not spoil my favorite stories. "The Queen of Sheba" is a beautiful idyl, and the things you have suggested are merely the framework for perfect prose and charming fancy.

JOHN (*repentant*): I know it, my dear. Aldrich is an artist in words. (*Confessing his duplicity.*) I often read his poetry—over and over again for the crystal beauty of it. There is never a halting foot, never a stumbling rhyme. I always feel when I have finished one of his poems that he has done it once for all—polished it to the final comma.

MARJORIE (*gushingly*): You dear fellow—I am not to marry a Philistine after all!

JOHN (*teasing*) :   Well, I'm not so sure of that.
I draw the line at "Baby Bell." As a profane friend
of mine often says, "No dead kids in my literature,
please."

MARJORIE (*wiping her eyes*) :   Why will you say
such disagreeable things ?—just when I begin to hope
for you.

JOHN (*making it up*) :   I must chaff now and then,
you know.   You may praise "Wyndham Towers,"
"Spring in New England," "Friar Jerome," and
"Pepita," all you wish, and I'll agree with you.

MARJORIE (*brightening*) :   Why, those are his very
best poems.   You really have some discernment.

JOHN (*self-satisfied*) :   Even a New York man
knows a perfect thing of its kind when it comes his
way.   When I read Aldrich I think of rare cameos
and intaglios.

MARJORIE :   There is less of handiwork and more
natural beauty in my impression.   I think of a lovely
opal where the richest tints and colors play—all the
beauty of the great arch of the sky, when the au-
rora waves over it, caught and imprisoned in that
little gem.

JOHN (*aside, reflectively*) :   I suppose that when
you really arouse a New England girl you find a
poet.   (*To* MARJORIE.)   But you have not mentioned
the best story of all, from a man's point of view—
"The Story of a Bad Boy."

MARJORIE.   Girls don't care to read about the
pranks of bad boys.   We suffer enough from them in

real life. (*A handsome young man on horseback turns up the driveway toward the house.*) There is the original Bad Boy now ! Don't you know Tom Bailey, of New York, the distinguished politician and editor ? He is at the Surf House. (*Greetings and introductions when* BAILEY *has dismounted.*) We were speaking of you. Mr. Flemming thinks your biography the best of Mr. Aldrich's novels.

BAILEY (*in despair*) : Can I never live down that awful tale of my youth ! Some people really believe that I did all those things. I think I should have been nominated for governor last June if a rival paper had not unearthed what it called my "Terrible Record as a Boy in Rivermouth."

FLEMMING (*laughing*) : I remember ; but I heard a dozen men at the club declare that they would like to have a chance to vote for the original of the Bad Boy. They all looked upon you as the friend of their youth. I haven't a doubt that every winter a wave of midnight explosions sweeps over the villages of this country. It means that the next crop of boys has been reading the " Story of a Bad Boy." It is passed along from generation to generation of village youngsters with "Tom Brown" and " Verdant Green." *That* is true immortality for an author. There are no books we love so long, no authors we remember so kindly as those we read and delighted in when young.

BAILEY (*with mock earnestness*) : Then I'm condemned to go down to posterity as the terror of good

33

parents and correct school-teachers.   I am even mistrusted by the village police everywhere !

MARJORIE (*cutting in*) :   But the village girls won't love you the less for it.

FLEMMING (*judiciously*) :   Aldrich did one very fine thing with the " Bad Boy; " he annihilated the prig in American juvenile literature for a generation.

MARJORIE :   And that's almost as good as being the delightful poet that he is.   (*A maid appears in the doorway.*)   And now we'll have luncheon.

(*Exeunt.*)

FRANK R. STOCKTON

THE LADY OR THE TIGER?

THE HOUSEHOLD OF FRANK R. STOCKTON

THE LADY, ... { One of the fairest maidens at a semi-barbaric court.

THE TIGER, ... The fiercest beast in the kingdom.

SCENE: *Two exactly similar adjoining rooms hung with the skins of wild beasts. A small iron-barred window in the centre of the dividing wall; heavily padded doors lead from each into a huge arena. In one room—*THE LADY; *in the other—*THE TIGER.

TIME: *The Present.*

THE LADY (*rousing from a deep sleep on a divan covered with leopard skins*) :

OH, I am weary, weary of this waiting! Here must I stay till that young man answers the conundrum, and chooses the Lady or the Tiger.

THE TIGER (*with his huge paws sticking through the iron bars of the window*) : Hello, there! You needn't make such a fuss about it; I'm in the same boat with you.

LADY (*satirically*) : But you're a tiger, and a man-tiger at that. You're used to the solitude of the jungle, while my only life has been the gayety of court. Why must we be shut up here all these years?

37

"HELLO, THERE!"

TIGER (*philosophically, scratching his left ear with his right paw*):
Well, it's all done for a good cause —the cause of literature. The slave who brought me my breakfast this morning said that he heard the king remark to his daughter, the other day, that if the question were settled about the Lady or the Tiger, Stockton's occupation as a story-writer would be gone.

LADY: I don't see why!

TIGER (*viciously*): Women never do.

LADY (*with severe dignity*): Perhaps Your Royal Bengal Highness can enlighten me?

TIGER: It's just this way: Every time Stockton publishes a new book, most of the people in the kingdom rush to buy it to see whether it contains the answer to the Lady or the Tiger conundrum. When they don't find the answer, they keep on hoping and buy the next book; and so on indefinitely.

LADY (*interested*): It isn't a bad scheme.

38

"OH, I AM WEARY, WEARY OF THIS WAITING!"

TIGER : A regular lead-pipe cinch. It does not matter what he writes, the people are bound to buy it.

LADY : Oh, well, they get their money's worth,

"THEY KEEP ON HOPING AND BUY THE NEXT BOOK."

anyhow. The Nubian maid who waits on me always brings me his new books. I get a great deal of fun out of them.

TIGER (*cynically*) : You have to ; you've nothing else to do, except to embroider that wedding-dress which you won't have a chance to wear.

LADY (*with tears in her eyes*) : It's mean of you to bully a poor, weak woman. You are like all the men I used to know ; they are half-tiger in their dispositions, the brutes.

TIGER (*showing his teeth*) : I don't feel flattered

39

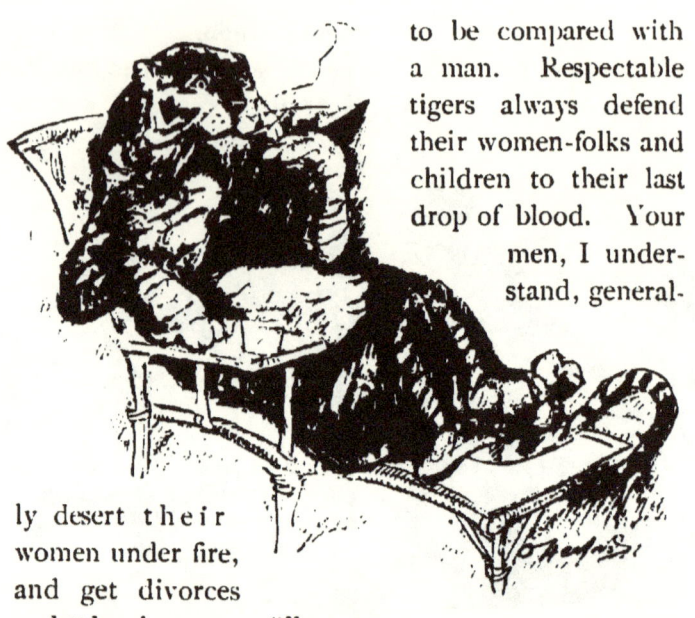

to be compared with a man. Respectable tigers always defend their women-folks and children to their last drop of blood. Your men, I understand, general-ly desert their women under fire, and get divorces and "legal separations," and break up their families, and let their cubs shift for themselves. We may bully our tigresses a good deal, but we are not *that* bad !

"YOU NEVER DO ANYTHING BUT SMOKE CIG-ARETTES AND READ RIDER HAGGARD."

LADY (*conciliating him*) : Well—you *have* a pretty good heart when one gets through your hide. But that *is* tough ! That is why I despair of ever improving your literary taste. So far as I can see through the grating, you never do anything but brush your royal stripes, smoke cigarettes, and read Rider Haggard.

TIGER (*with a leer*) : Well, isn't that better than reading Stockton's everlasting conundrums?

LADY (*patronizingly*) : You just show your ignorance !   Mr. Stockton has written some perfectly beautiful tales with no conundrums in them at all.   There is " Mrs. Lecks and Mrs. Aleshine."

TIGER (*cutting in*) :   I guess The Dusantes were the conundrum in that book !

LADY (*protesting*) :   But he answered that in the sequel.   Then there is " The Late Mrs. Null "——

TIGER (*with a fiendish laugh*) :   The biggest conundrum of the lot !   I tell you Stockton is simply a great big **?**

LADY (*pettishly*) :   I won't talk to you any more to-day, unless you play fair.   (*Coaxingly.*)   But isn't " Rudder Grange " perfectly splendid ?   Come now, you must admit that !

TIGER (*dubiously, chewing his claws*) :   I'm not saying that I was not interested in that, the day you poked it through the bars.   *Pomona* and *Euphemia*, and the canal-boat, are great fun.   But the *men* are such awful idiots !   There may be men like those, but I never knew a genteel tiger who was such a fool.

LADY (*brightening up*) :   And you did enjoy reading about *Pomona's* daughter, and the baby borrowed from New Dublin, and *Lord Edward* ?

TIGER (*reluctantly*) :   Oh, yes ! But they're not a patch on " King Solomon's Mines."

LADY (*in despair*) :   You are

41

such a bloodthirsty creature—like a real man. The only way to lead a man clear through a book is with a trail of gore. Why can't you appreciate nice, quiet, gentle humor, full of good-will and sunshine, like Mr. Stockton's? I don't believe he ever spoiled a page of a book with a grewsome or disagreeable image. That is why we women read so much of him. He soothes our nerves.

TIGER (*maliciously*) : That's the business of pills —not literature.

LADY (*indignantly*) : You are incorrigible, and I won't talk to you. Go away from that window !

TIGER (*diplomatically*) : Come, my dear lady, I have a great scheme to propose to you—a final solution of the conundrum of the Lady or the Tiger !

LADY (*resignedly*) : All right ; I'll listen. Anything is better than staying here longer.

TIGER : I'm glad to hear you say that, for you'll be sure to accept my plan. You know that every day at twelve o'clock, for ten years, that young man who loved the princess is brought into the arena to choose one of these two doors—the Lady or the Tiger. Well, the king and the law can't compel him to choose till he's ready, and he won't be ready till he sees a perfectly untroubled smile on the princess's countenance when she points out the door. Do you follow me ?

LADY : Perfectly. For ten years he has been afraid to trust her to point out the door. And if he knows her disposition as well as I do he never will

42

trust her. She'd rather have him *die* than marry me !

TIGER (*with joy*) : That's it, exactly. What I have to propose gets around that beautifully. You see, these bars are near enough together to keep me from jumping through, but they are far enough apart for a *petite* woman like you to crawl through. Now, if you will kindly put that hassock under the window, and stand on it, I'll pull you through with my paws. Then I'll gently eat you—you are pretty enough to eat, and I'll be very nice about it ; I shan't even wrinkle your gown. To-morrow morning, when the Nubian maid comes, she'll find your cell empty, and will immediately report to the princess. The princess will keep it to herself, and, at noon, when the young man is brought into the arena, she will joyfully point toward your door, which he will open with a great show of bravery. Of course *you* will not be there, and the king will think that the gods have settled the question, for there won't be any traces of you ; and then he will order that I be released in my native jungles, and that the young man and the princess be immediately married. There you are, everybody pleased and happy, and the great conundrum solved !

LADY (*hurling the hassock at the win-*

43

dow) :   You horrid, horrid creature!   You must have got that idea from one of Rider Haggard's awful books !

Tiger :   Meouw—wow—wow !

RICHARD HARDING DAVIS

THE HOUSEHOLD OF
RICHARD HARDING DAVIS

Van Bibber, ...	A gentleman of leisure.
Eleanore Cuyler, . . .	{ Devoted to society and good works.
The Other Woman, . .	Quite " impossible " in Our Set.
Gallegher, ...	} A young tough, with good impulses.

Scene: *A Green car on Broadway above Twenty-third Street; time, two o'clock on an August afternoon. The streets are almost deserted. The only occupant of the car is a tastefully dressed young woman who is absorbed in reading a letter.*

(*Enter* Van Bibber, *puffing a little.*)

CHARMED to catch a glimpse of you in town in midsummer; was waiting a few hours, on my way from Newport, to hear from my yacht which is somewhere between here and Oyster Bay. Caught sight of your profile in the car window and ran for it. Awfully jolly to have the town all to ourselves like this. Account for yourself, please ?

Miss Cuyler: I came down to consult, for a few

47

hours, with the girls at the College Settlement on Rivington Street. You know I am on the Advisory Committee, and we occasionally have difficult questions to solve; they've put an unusually hard one to me in this letter.

VAN BIBBER : Sorry I can't offer to help you ; but I always mix things up. No head for fine questions of morals. (*Grasping for an idea.*) I have it, hah, hah. Ask our friend Dickey, hah, hah. He is always giving the girls good advice.

MISS CUYLER : Oh, is Mr. Davis in town ? I thought he was abroad.

VAN BIBBER : He was ; just arrived yesterday on the *Paris*. No end of new togs—lovely coaching coat that touches his heels—beautiful collars with a sheer to them like a racing yacht—a new shade in gloves, and all that sort of thing.

MISS CUYLER : I don't doubt he is stunning, but that won't solve my difficulty.

VAN BIBBER (*showing*

48

his disappointment) : I thought you were one of his disciples ?

MISS CUYLER : I have read all his stories, even the one about myself. (*Looking quiz-zically at* VAN BIBBER.) Do you think he has quite done us justice, Mr. Van Bibber ?

VAN BIBBER (*a little confused*) : Oh, I say, you must not tease. I'm not the man he put in those stories, really now—a mere coincidence in names. You don't think I'd do that ridiculous " swan-boat " business, do you ? Never took so much trouble for anybody in my life, never.

MISS CUYLER : I am not so sure of that. You are more of a man than you like most people to think.

VAN BIBBER (*laughing*) : Chaff — more chaff— you're always chaffing me. (*Confidentially.*) But frankly now, Miss Cuyler, I'm not the sort of a cad he put in those stories, am I ? I don't pose as such a dreadfully superior person, do I, and patronize peo-ple who are less lucky than I am ?

MISS CUYLER (*sincerely*) : No, no ; you are never that. The only thing I don't like about you is your accent, and that's improving. Where *did* you pick it up ?

VAN BIBBER (*honestly*) : In England. Thought it was the real thing, and have just found out that it is cockney. (*Ingenuously.*) I say, now—you—you don't mind my telling you that *you* are nicer than the girl in Dickey's story?

MISS CUYLER (*with a sidelong glance*): I've always known that. We New York girls are not half the prigs he takes us to be. One might think from his stories that we are a combination of gorgeous frocks and intense sentiments—a sort of virtuous *Camille*, if you can imagine that type.

VAN BIBBER: Horribly disagreeable type to live with—always want to know the reason Why for every action. Dramatize their emotions and their friends, and want you to live up to their play. But you are——

MISS CUYLER (*cutting in*): Oh, I know. We are sensible enough. The New York girl is the product of very practical conditions. It is in the blood. Our fathers may have inherited their wealth but our grandfathers made it, and most of them in a very humble way. That sort of thing isn't forgotten in a generation.

VAN BIBBER: Most of the girls I know are good fellows.

MISS CUYLER: They have to be, or their brothers would make their lives miserable.

VAN BIBBER: But Dickey looks at you through a kind of literary atmosphere. His stories are——

MISS CUYLER (*interrupting*): " New York from a Car Window " would be a good title for them.

VAN BIBBER (*a little cynically*): Next season I

suppose we'll have " London from a Car Window," and then Paris, and so on around the world.

MISS CUYLER : Come now. Aren't we a little cruel to one of our best friends? He has a wonderfully good narrative style, at any rate, and he never wastes words in telling a story.

VAN BIBBER : Yes; and I don't think he is ever dull. You know he *sees things*—and that's a good deal.

MISS CUYLER (*meditatively*) : He sees a great deal and he has an eye for the dramatic effect of things. Color and composition are his literary weapons.

VAN BIBBER : And very few use them so well. Most of our story-writers simply think they are thinking.

MISS CUYLER (*glancing out of the car window toward a corner of the street*) : Do you see that woman in half mourning, standing on the crossing and waiting for this car ? *That* is to be the answer to my question from the College Settlement.

VAN BIBBER (*who knows the town*) : By Jove, that is the Other Woman of Dickey's story, on account of whom our friend Miss Ellen threw over Latimer. Where did you meet her ?

MISS CUYLER : Down at the Settlement a few

months ago. She is absorbed in good work of that kind. Run along now, and let me talk with her.

VAN BIBBER (*going out as the car stops. Under his breath*) : Whew ! To think that the dashing Birdie Benson should have taken to the Church !

(*Enter* THE OTHER WOMAN, *who is recognized by* MISS CUYLER. *They sit together and talk.*)

MISS CUYLER : The girls have written to me that you want to join in our work actively, and I am on my way to talk with them about it.

THE OTHER WOMAN : That is my errand also, and I am glad that I met you here alone where I can make an explanation. I don't want to go into this work while you have a false impression in your mind about me.

MISS CUYLER : Your frankness wins me.

THE OTHER WOMAN : I need all of your good-will, oh, more than you can imagine. You must know first that I am not what you think me. I am not a widow ; I am not even a wife. (*With hesitation.*) I came from a home of refinement in a country village. It is the old story of a trusting girl deceived by the glib phrases of a city man of a certain type. My evil genius was a man of your own circle —handsome, plausible, almost eloquent. He has the fatal faculty of deceiving himself as easily as he deceives others. We were very happy for a time in a fool's Paradise, until he met a young woman in

52

"THE OTHER WOMAN OF DICKEY'S STORY."

society, the daughter of a bishop, whom he thought worthy of his superior qualities. Then he came to me with one of his canting sermons about his " duty to himself, his family, and society," and threw me over like a toy of which he was tired. He really loved me sincerely, too.

MISS CUYLER (*aside*): I always thought that Latimer's remarks to the bishop in his study were solemn nonsense, and now I know it. You can trust a woman like Ellen for seeing through a sham every time.

THE OTHER WOMAN (*continuing*): The rest of my story is very short, but it is the worst. All my good impulses were dried up by his cruelty, and I plunged into a world of which you do not even dream, and led a life that gained me the nickname of the " Dash-ing Birdie Benson." But one cannot escape from the good influences of the home of one's youth, and for a year now they have been drawing me to better things.

MISS CUYLER : You poor child. I am sorry for

55

you with all my heart. You must go away from this city where your old career will surely find you out. I'll discover a way out of it all.

(*Enter newsboy with papers.*)

GALLEGHER : Poypers ! Here's yer evenin' poypers ! *Telegram, Nooes, Worl'*, an' *Sun !*

MISS CUYLER (*scrutinizingly*) : Aren't you Mr. Davis's friend, Gallegher, who caught the murderer over in Philadelphia ?

GALLEGHER (*with a grin*) : Yep ; I'm from Phillie. It's too slow a town for me. But that's a lot of guff he's been a-givin' ye, about me an' the bruisers. I got onto the bloke wid only tree fingers to his hand, but I didn't do no cry-baby and holy cherub act when the coppers chased me into the *Press* office. I slid up to the managing editor and said, " Here's Mr. Dwyer's copy. Rush it quick. And say, cully, can't ye give me a box of cigarettes for bringing it so soon ? " That's all that's uv it. See ! (*Exit, singing*) EXTRY. Full account of the Tornady !

(*Conductor yells " Rivington Street," and both exeunt.*)

F. MARION CRAWFORD

THE HOUSEHOLD OF F. MARION CRAWFORD

Mr. Isaacs, ...	{ A learned Persian, dealer in precious stones.
Ram Lal, ...	An " adept " in Buddhism.
Russell Vanbrugh, . . .	A New York lawyer.
Princess Saracinesca, . .	Of the Italian nobility.

SCENE : *The deck of a P. & O. steamer bound for Bombay, on the Indian Ocean ; a smooth sea, a gently moving warm breeze, and a brilliant tropical night. People of all nationalities are promenading the decks, and amidships there is music and dancing. In the shelter of the deck-cabins aft, a little group is seated apart in earnest discussion.*

PRINCESS SARACINESCA : Oh the beauty of this tropic night ! It is the sky of Italy with the stars intensified.

VANBRUGH : More volts of electricity in the heavenly lamps.

ISAACS : You Americans measure beauty in commercial terms. I never knew but one of you who was an idealist—and that was years ago in Simla.

VANBRUGH : What is the name of the Prodigy?

ISAACS : Marion Crawford—a journalist in India when I knew him, but now a popular novelist. For years he has sent me all his books.

59

PRINCESS :   I often meet him in Rome——
VANBRUGH :   And I in New York.

ISAACS :   And each of us no doubt finds him perfectly at home—a true cosmopolite, a citizen of the
world.   He is an excellent example of my theory that
the more a man sees and knows, the more of an idealist he becomes.   Such a man sees widely different
realities standing for an expression of the same mental or spiritual truth.   They become to his clear eye
the mere foliage of truth which varies with the acci-
dents of climate, environment, nationality.   The
great writers of romance, in poetry or prose, have
been always men of wide knowledge of the world—
Scott, Dumas, Hugo.

VANBRUGH : But a New England school-mistress whose horizon is bounded by her village streets will always write realistic stories.

ISAACS (*waving his hand toward the promenaders*) : How can any one look at this moving throng—the nations of the world in microcosm—and doubt that the essence of life is the unseen—the ideal ! I have seen into the heart of yonder Buddhist, in his strange robe, and know that it has throbbed with like aspirations to mine. When you find what you once thought to be a mere vision of your imagination equally domesticated under the fez of a Turk, the turban of a Hindoo, and the pot hat of an Englishman, you begin to suspect that the things which are seen are temporal, and those which are unseen are eternal. That is what Crawford has put into his romances—the marvellous heart of man of whatever nation or tongue, torn with the same longings and desires, soothed with the same hopes. And yet learned men are saying that this is not the age of romance !

PRINCESS (*earnestly*) : As I have grown older and have had leisure to read and travel more, it has been driven home to me that what we call Romance is the highest realism. The very wonders of industry, science, invention, which we call the spirit of the age, are the romantic dreams of strong men made visible.

VANBRUGH : But that does not justify the impossible romances of Crawford. A cynical friend of mine calls them " fairy tales for grown-up children."

PRINCESS : Why " fairy tales ! " What is every-day New York to you—the telephone, the phonograph, the Elevated, the Brooklyn Bridge—would surpass the wildest dreams of impossible things that ever entered the head of that Arab trader who came on board at Aden. Go tell him that at home you talk to a friend a thousand miles away in a whisper, and hear the voice of your father who is dead repeated from a waxen spool ! He will laugh in your face—but will add that if you want to hear a true story of marvellous things he will tell you the tale of Aladdin's Lamp.

VANBRUGH : I don't object to one of Crawford's rattling stories when I want to be amused after a hard day in court—but then you must not ask me to take that sort of thing seriously. (*Smiling.*) I don't believe he takes it seriously himself.

ISAACS : That is beside the point. What I have been trying to say is that the so-called Romantic attitude toward life is nearer truth than the Realistic. When Crawford writes romances he is attempting a higher form of art than—say Zola.

PRINCESS : The striking thing to me in his work is that, while his attitude toward life is romantic, his stage-setting is always realistic. Saracinesca and I have been everywhere in recent years, and we have found the descriptions in Mr. Crawford's books almost photographic—Constantinople, Munich, Prague, Arabia, London, New York, and our dear Italy.

ISAACS: I am glad to hear you say that. Romance is no excuse for lazy or inaccurate observation. The best romancers are as accurate as the realists.

PRINCESS: Stevenson, Bourget, Loti, Kipling— for other examples at the present time—all travelling the world over for impressions of men and things !

VANBRUGH: I care little for your distinctions of schools, method, and attitude. You are simply talking the slang of art. But as a practical man with some experience in sifting the motives of men, I have often found Crawford's novels deficient in character-drawing. His men are all enormously rich, clever, and handsome; his women are surpassingly beautiful, and they all speak in the florid language of the melodrama.

ISAACS: I prefer the language which clearly mirrors the thought, even though florid, to the linguistic horrors which some of your writers have put in what I believe you call dialect stories. I picked up a volume of them in the hotel reading-room at Cairo the other day. It is my good fortune

LOTI.

to know something of twenty languages — and yet never have I come across anything so strange as those

63

tales. A young American girl came looking for the book which she had forgotten, and I asked her to tell me what it was. "My Royal Princelet," she said, with a bewitching smile, "we call that the great, native American literature, in the States. We are proud of it, and each section of the country booms its own dialect poet or novelist along with its wheat-acreage and output of pig-iron."

TRAVELS WITH A DONKEY.

VANBRUGH (*laughing*): Does your philosophy account for the American girl?

ISAACS (*with a puzzled look*): I meet her everywhere in my travels, and she is more mysterious to me than my Buddhist teacher and seer, Ram Lal.

(*The moon rises slowly out of the water, and as its first rays break over the side of the vessel an aged Buddhist appears.*)

RAM LAL: Peace, Abdul Hafiz! You spoke my name.

ISAACS: Aleikum Salaam, Ram Lal! My friends and I have been talking about the young American who once was with us in the Himalayan Mountains on a perilous mission.

RAM LAL: A brave man, my brother, and a teller of strange tales which I have since read in books on

64

the market-stalls of Cairo, Suez, and Bombay. I should rather read his books than argue with him, for I found him something of a sophist. As I have often said, " Life is too short to argue."

Isaacs : But you did not find his books sophistical ?

Ram Lal : Nay, my brother, for I have found in them the sincerity that dwells only in the heart. Now the heart of man is the seed-ground for the flowers of the spirit. In it are planted those aspirations which under a quickening influence may spring into vigorous life. But wonderful as the heart is in its possibilities, it still belongs to the earth, and our friend's beautiful stories are of the earth. The fidelity, the heroism, the beauty in them are of the world, worldly. The idealism in them is artistic idealism, and has nothing akin to the highest idealism which is essen-

65

tially moral.   Higher than the laws of romance are the laws of Nature, which are the laws of Buddha. The essence of them is not pleasure, or beauty, or fidelity to the affections, but Self-sacrifice.   (*As a fleecy cloud obscures the moon, he fades away*): *calling* Peace be with you !

ISAACS :   And with you.   Peace !
(All arise in silence and start below.)

VANBRUGH (*aside*):   That old boy talks like a transcendental summer-school of Philosophy.   They might appreciate him at Concord, but he's one too many for me.   I'm rather glad Crawford isn't chuck full of " moral idealism."   Think I'll go below and finish " Marion Darche " before I turn in.

(*Exit.*)

RUDYARD KIPLING

" Show me the face of Truth," the Sahib said—
" Show me its beauty, before I'm dead ! "
" Look ! " said the priest, " with unflinching eyes ;
" This is the World, and not Paradise.
" Look ! It is wicked, and cruel, and strong, and wise ! "
—A Buddhist Seer.

MRS. HAUKSBEE, ...	{ Admired by men and feared by women.
CAPTAIN GADSBY, ...	Of the Pink Hussars.
MISS THREEGAN, ...	Engaged to Captain Gadsby.
TERENCE MULVANEY, . . .	{ Private in B Company of the Old Regiment.

SCENE : *Veranda of the Threegan house at Simla. A fine view of the Simla hills and the valley below.* MISS THREEGAN *is seated in a long chair, her eyes on the distant hills and her thoughts in England. In her lap an open letter of many sheets, bearing the London post-mark. Her revery is broken in upon by footsteps of " a big yellow man with an enormous moustache," who walks with a cavalry swagger.*

TIME : *A hot afternoon.*

CAPTAIN GADSBY : Ha—hmmm !

MISS THREEGAN (*coming back from England and the hills with reluctance*) : Is that all you have to say ?

GADSBY : Come now, dear, be kind to me. I

know you like this hour to yourself, but the club's deserted and all Simla is taking its afternoon nap, and I'm desperately lonely. Dear old Mafflin has just gone back to the plains and I miss him awful.

Miss Threegan (*pettishly*) : I half believe you care more for that Captain Mafflin than you do for me, and, when we're married, I won't have it (*tapping her foot*). I *won't* have it, sir.

Gadsby (*conciliating*) : I say, little featherweight, you won't be hard on Jack, will you? He saved my life at Amdheran. If it had not been for Jack, sweetheart, you'd be engaged to another man.

Miss Threegan (*indignantly*) : Never! How dare you hint at such a thing? We were *always* intended for each other. It was pre—pre——

Gadsby : Predestinated, and Jack was the divine instrument. So there!

Miss Threegan : Oh, well, you may still care for Jack a little, if you'll let me always love dear Emma, and tell her all my secrets.

Gadsby : What, that little Deercourt thing who used to make fun of me to my face? Never, never! She's in England, isn't she, now?

Miss Threegan : Yes, and this is a lovely, long letter from her. Do you know, Pip, I think she's in love with Captain Mafflin—just a little bit?

Gadsby (*with warmth*) : The little minx—hardly out of the nursery and short dresses. Outrageous. Why, Jack is a *man*, dear, a big brave man.

Miss Threegan (*shyly*) : Emma may be a little

Miss Threegan.

minx and a nursery child with an *ayah*, but she is one year older than the young woman you expect to marry, sir. Now what have you got to say for yourself?

GADSBY (*cornered*) : By Jove, little one, there's only one apology. (*Loving interlude.*) Now, tell me all about Emma's letter—she's a dear girl, and Jack must marry her. (*Fiercely.*) I'll compel him to it.

MISS THREEGAN (*mollified*) : She writes that she is having a beautiful time in London ; and who do you think is the literary lion of the season ?

GADSBY : Couldn't guess. Never read books.

MISS THREEGAN : But it's an old friend of yours.

GADSBY : No friend of mine ever wrote anything but beastly, dull official reports.

MISS THREEGAN : Well, then, stupid, it's Mr. Kipling !

GADSBY (*with astonishment*) : What ! Not dear Ruddy, the boy who did those ballads and things for the *Military Gazette ?* Awfully good fellow, you know ; but Ruddy can't make literature. Why, those stories of his in the *Gazette* were simply photographs of what we all see around us here. Everybody knows that—true to life to the last button. *That* isn't what they call literature.

MISS THREEGAN (*laughing at him*) : You're a dear old goose. You've just said the best thing possible in his praise. All England and America are talking about his stories, because they have revealed

73

a new world to them "true to life to the last button."

GADSBY: There's Mrs. Hauksbee! Let us call
her in and tell her. She always said Ruddy would
be a great man. Wonderful woman, that! (*Calling
to* MRS. HAUKSBEE *who is going by in a 'Rickshaw.*)
Come and have a cup of tea; we've good news to
tell you!

MRS. HAUKSBEE (*trips up the lawn and sits in a*

hammock, fanning) : I wanted to stop, but I did not like to interrupt a pair of lovers.

GADSBY (*with clumsy gallantry*) : You're never an interruption, Mrs. Hauksbee. (MISS THREEGAN *scowls a little while she pours tea.*) Did you know that Kipling had taken London by storm ? Literary lion and all that sort of thing.

MRS. HAUKSBEE (*who is never surprised at any-thing*) : I've been expecting it. I said to him : " My dear boy, fill your pockets with those stories of yours from the *Gazette ;* go to England and make a book out of them. You'll show them at home for the first time what sort of an Empire they are govern-ing. An Englishman likes to be hit from the shoulder, and that is your style. You'll hit him." Rud stroked his big chin a moment, rubbed his glasses, and said : " I'll try it. I'll call the book ' Plain Tales from the Hills,' and dedicate it ' To the Wittiest Woman in India.' " He always was a neat man at flattery.

MISS THREEGAN (*with severity*) : I must say I think many of his stories in the *Gazette* were wicked —very, very wicked. The men use such horrible language.

MRS. HAUKSBEE (*looking at* GADSBY *with a glitter in her eyes*) : But, my sweet child, you must not judge all men by the beautiful language of Captain Gadsby. Some of them *do* use horrid words when they are with each other.

GADSBY (*whose vocabulary is famous at the club*) :

75

Ha—hmmm! Yes, indeed, Minnie—the men do occasionally talk like that. Ruddy lived with us and knew the slang. (*Aside.*) I'll fine him a magnum and a score of pegs, when I catch him back here, for giving the boys away so dreadfully.

MISS THREEGAN (*blushing a little*): But the women, Mrs. Hauksbee! They do such terrible things in those stories. Ugh. I don't think this world is very, very bad.

MRS. HAUKSBEE (*stabbing at* GADSBY): You must always believe what the Captain tells you about the world, when you are married.

GADSBY (*thinking about Mrs. Herriott down at Naini Tal, and what she will say when he breaks it to her that he is engaged*): There are wicked women in India, too, my dear—a good many of them. (*Humbly.*) But it mostly isn't their fault; it's the men. We are often brutes. (*Aside.*) What a dashed brute I've been to *that* woman.

MRS. HAUKSBEE (*with more sincerity than usual*): I think that Kipling has put our inmost souls on paper, and that is why we squirm. I often told him he should shut his eyes to what is unpleasant, and see more of the ideal and beautiful. But he would glare at me through the upper half of his glasses, square his jaw another degree, and laugh in my eyes. By and by he would say, quizzically: " Well, don't I see what is really and honestly fine in a man like Mulvaney, or Learoyd, or Gaddy ; or in a woman whom I won't name in your presence ; or in boys like Lew and Jakin." (*Looking at* GADSBY.) And I've had to acknowledge it, and say : "You are a poet, my little man, but you see too much." Then he would look far away to the snow-line of the hills and say, sadly, but with determination : "I won't be driven by nice scruples into praising those things which most people think fine and virtuous simply because they are conventional. I won't, I won't. Some day I'll write a poem about a man named Tomlinson, who could be admitted neither to heaven nor hell when he died, because he had no original virtues or no original vices. He was simply conventional, and so they sent him back to London to be happy." What can you say to a man who talks to you like that, Captain Gadsby ?

GADSBY (*who is a judge of men*) : Nothing. By Jove, I believe he's got a hold of the right end of things.

MRS. HAUKSBEE (*with conviction*) : So do I. And the critics may call him bumptious, and grotesque, and brutal, and vulgar, and all the other adjectives which they use for what is simply *unconventional ;* but I'll always believe that he has the heart of a man and the voice of a poet. The world does not often get the two united with such force. Oh, it is good to read what a strong man has written. Writing is mostly left to the weak who like to talk about their own emotions. Kipling looks at things like a man of action, and that's the great thing in life or letters.

GADSBY: Yes, he has *lived* with us, with all kinds of us—and that is why. There is a verse of his scrawled in charcoal over the grill in the Degchi Club which tells it all:

> " I have eaten your bread and salt,
> I have drunk your water and wine.
> The deaths ye died I have watched beside,
> And the lives that ye led were mine."

Why, would you believe it, there are three common soldiers down in B Company who would whip the regiment if Kipling asked them to! (*Pointing.*) There's one of them now, teaching the colonel's boy how to ride a pony. (*Calling.*) Mulvaney! Mulvaney! Bring the boy in. The ladies want to see him. (MULVANEY, *the boy, and the pony come up the broad roadway to the veranda, and at the regulation distance, salute. The boy has the precision of a veteran.*)

MULVANEY: It's only respict for you, Captain, that would lade me to inthurrupt the mornin' drill uv the mounted battalion.

GADSBY: We want to tell you of an old friend of yours— Mr. Kipling. He's become a great man at home, in England, writing for them all about India.

MULVANEY.

MULVANEY: God bless him:

78

he's a broth uv a man. Many's the peg he's dhrunk wid me an' Jock and Stanley. Ses he, "Mulvaney, soom day I'll be for a writin' doon thim tales thot ye've been blandanderin' to me fur years past." And faith, if he's ben doin' that in London, there's little left betune Terence Mulvaney and dis-ris-pectability by this time. Dinah Shadd will mek uv me life a basted purgathory if she hears ut. (*Looking at* Miss Threegan.) Whin ye write to London, Miss, will ye say to Mister Kipling that the ould rig'mint is dhrinkin' health an' succis to him—three fingers, standin' up! (*Salutes. Then to boy on pony.*) 'Shun! By foors, right wheel, march! (*Exeunt, singing.*)

"And when the war began, we chased the bold Afghan, An' we made the bloomin' Ghazi for to flee, boys O!"

Mrs. Hauksbee (*thoughtfully*): It's because Rud knew men like that, and like you—and all of us from Viceroy to *Sais*, that he is able to write so truthfully, so vividly, that men and women ten thousand miles away feel that they have lived here among us. (*Summons her 'Rickshaw, and all rise to walk down the lawn.*)

GEORGE MEREDITH

"That kindly man in grey homespun who sits in his little châlet on the hillside yonder, and writes great books."

THE HOUSEHOLD OF GEORGE MEREDITH

NEVIL BEAUCHAMP, . . . Commander R. N. and a Radical.
ADRIAN HARLEY, ... A Wise Youth and a cynic.
DIANA WARWICK, ... Of the Crossways, Surrey.
TOM REDWORTH, ... ⎰ An English gentleman, engaged
⎱ to Diana.

SCENE: *The ridge of Box Hill in Surrey, from which spreads a wonderful view. The spires of Dorking in the middle distance; on the right a great rise of wooded hills, dotted with country places, with a glimpse of the village of Guildford. The hills and valleys are flooded with the sunshine of a perfect June day. DIANA and REDWORTH are seated on a rustic bench near the winding pathway along which pass and repass groups on their way to the summit of Box Hill.*

D IANA : After all my storms and shipwreck, Tom, you have towed the derelict into this bay of green and peaceful hills.

REDWORTH (*pointing across the valley*): And there, in the clump of trees near Guildford, is The Crossways—your safe anchorage always.

DIANA : And I shall never slip the anchor—never again without you as pilot. The world is a great sea, beautiful and tempestuous—and, oh so cruel to a woman alone! (*looking in his eyes*). I am glad that you are so strong a man, and that you love me.

83

REDWORTH : All the years that I have waited for you are a little day, and an hour like this is a lifetime.

DIANA (*smiling*) : And this is my quiet, prosaic Tom, who never spoke a word of love to me in all these years, but always fought my battles !

REDWORTH : If you are glad that I have been persistent in loving you, Diana, you must thank that kindly man in grey homespun who sits in his little châlet on the hillside yonder, and writes great books.

DIANA : So it is Mr. Meredith who has been making my everyday Tom a poet—and not love at all ? We women always find that a man is the inspiration of those best things which we flatter ourselves that we have inspired.

REDWORTH (*solemnly*) : Since the night of that ball in Dublin, when I first saw " the flashing arrows in your eyes," I have had but one inspiration—the love of you. But one day when I was in despair about your loving Dacier, and was walking gloomily across

the downs I met Meredith at the crossing of a hedge. He caught the trouble in my eyes, and we sat down on the top step of the stile to talk it out. " My boy," he said when he had heard it all, " no one can love as you love without eternal profit to your soul—whether in the

84

"And there, in the clump of trees near Guildford, is The Crossways."

end you win her or not. It is the strength of Nature in you creating an ideal which has given and will always give a unity and stability to your work. I never see a man successful in the right way (not by luck or selfishness)—a man who is doing strenuously the best that Nature has put in him to do —that I do not begin to look for the *one idea* which is the inspiration of it. I have watched your life and work here and in London for ten years—your steady, persistent development—and have often wondered what the main-spring was. Now I *know* it ! Go on, go on, and the very laws of Nature, which are the laws of God, will fight for you ! " Then he strode across the downs, his grey eyes filled with that soft light which Nature gives to those who love her.

DIANA (*reflecting*) : He met my Tom a despairing lover and left him a brave man ! Mr. Meredith is always putting heart and hope into thoughtful men and women everywhere. What a lovely afternoon his life is having—belated fame come home at last, the admiration of intellectual people, the love of friends.

REDWORTH (*pointing down the pathway*) : There are two of his friends now—as different as men can be ; both well-born—the one an enthusiast, a reformer, a radical ; the other *blasé* and a cynic. Yet if you go deep enough (as Meredith no doubt has) you will find a common substratum which makes them congenial—the cynic and the reformer both love humanity. The cynic jeers at one side of it—its frailties ; the reformer lauds another side of it—its common

virtues. Each in his own heart loves that middle
ground where frailties and virtues mingle—and *that*
is ordinary human nature.

(*Enter* BEAUCHAMP *and* ADRIAN.)

BEAUCHAMP (*greeting* DIANA *and* REDWORTH):
At the foot of the hill we passed Meredith standing by
his box-wood hedge. He waved a hand and called
out to us, " Follow that path up the hill and you'll
find Happiness; a little while ago I saw two lovers
go by, hand in hand." (DIANA *looks consciously at*
REDWORTH.) And Adrian jeers back at him, " No
happiness ever came from following Love. This is
the hill of Purgatory." " With Dante's Beatrice at
the top," called Meredith. " Rather a Siren whis-
tling from a rock," ungallantly jibed Adrian ; and so
we passed out of hearing with our game of " Shuttle-
cock."

DIANA (*to* ADRIAN): Still playing at cynic, O
Wise Youth, while the rest of the world moves on to
happiness.

ADRIAN (*to* DIANA): For you " the rest of the
world " is simply Redworth.

DIANA (*bowing*): If you could see " the rest of
the world " in one woman that I know you would
cease being a cynic. You know Mr. Meredith says
of you, " Adrian only sees one part of the world, and
that not the best part."

ADRIAN: Meredith is a howling optimist. He
sits on the hillside in his châlet and blows gorgeous

88

bubbles which mirror this lovely valley ; and he calls them the world, because they are round, and beautiful, and shot with rainbows.

DIANA (*pointedly*) : But Adrian is a jeering pessimist. He sits in his tower at Raynham Abbey, shuts out all the light, turns his eye inward on the memories of his youth, and says : " This is the world. It is full of high hopes which lead to nothing ; of false women and designing men ; of the dreams of a man of intellect that never produce action. All this is the world, and I'll laugh at it." Oh, Wise Youth, how much you could learn from Meredith !

BEAUCHAMP (*catching the last sentence*) : Learn from Meredith ! He has been my University. I never knew what it was to have any interests outside of my own people and class until I read him and talked with him. Men of letters are always praising his epigrams, his fancy, his imagination. They miss his greatness entirely. Meredith is great because he has put the very Spirit of Liberty in his creations. It is not Radicalism, or Socialism, or Liberalism ; it is the *attitude of mind* which is back of these and all other movements toward a broader life for all men. It is *individualism*.

DIANA : His first rule of freedom is to break the shackles which other men have forged for you.

ADRIAN : And then he puts on you a pair of his own particular kind of shackles ; I know the trick of the real philosopher. He prates of freedom—which

89

means liberty to make other people think as he himself thinks. That is the basis of all intellectual tyranny.

BEAUCHAMP: Meredith has no shackles. He says to every man: "Fall back on Nature for guidance—not landscapes and the mountains which are the Wordsworthian panacea—but your own nature in right conditions."

ADRIAN: To what awful depths it leads some men !

BEAUCHAMP: Because they and their fathers have been bound hand and foot for generations, and Nature has been distorted. For all these there is but one remedy—restore the conditions of Nature, freedom to work at what is congenial, freedom to live in God's pure air, freedom to know your fellowman on equal terms ! If that is socialism, I am a socialist and so is Meredith. We are better called simply humanitarians.

ADRIAN (*to* DIANA) : We must divert Beauchamp or we'll be getting a flood of his campaign speeches on us. (*To* BEAUCHAMP) I'll follow you in your admiration for Meredith on another tack. His epigrams charm me. He is one of the few contemporary writers of fiction who presuppose that their readers are beings of independent intelligence. His epigrams are flints which will only strike fire against steel.

DIANA : To me the finest thing in his work is his knowledge of a woman's heart. Other novelists,

even great ones, have made their women either delicate creatures of sentiment, or woolly-minded men in
petticoats. It has been beyond them to picture sentiment and strength united in a charming woman.
But Mr. Meredith has raised the standard of woman-
hood in fiction by women like Rosamund, Lucy,
Rhoda Fleming, Vittoria, Jenny Denham, and my
dearest Emmy.

ADRIAN: Wise Meredith! He flatters your sex
and you love him, and read his books.

REDWORTH (*quietly*): You have all had your say
about him, and have missed his best achievement.
Every one of his books teaches that the true social
unit is not a strong man alone, or an acute woman
alone—but a man and a woman who love each other
with all their hearts. That is Nature's greatest lesson. And all the barriers which caste, or prejudice,
or creed place between loving hearts are the foes of
progress. Break them down, Beauchamp; break
them down, Adrian! It isn't optimism, or pessim-
ism, or individualism that rules the world. It is
Love!

ADRIAN (*bowing to* DIANA *and* REDWORTH): I
salute the Social Unit, and continue my way alone
up the mountain of Purgatory. (*Starts up the pathway.*)

BEAUCHAMP: And I follow and hope to find
Beatrice at the summit. (*Exit.*)

DIANA (*calling after*): Her name is Jenny Denham, and I hope you'll find her.

REDWORTH : Come, dear, the shadow of the mountain has fallen on The Crossways, and we have a long walk across the valley before sunset.

(*They go down the Ridge of Box Hill.*)

"Come, dear, the shadow of the mountain has fallen on
The Crossways."

ROBERT LOUIS STEVENSON

"NOT TRULY ONE, BUT TRULY TWO."

THE HOUSEHOLD OF
ROBERT LOUIS STEVENSON

ALAN BRECK, ...	A Highland Jacobite of 1750.
DAVID BALFOUR, . .	A Young Lowland Scot.
DR. JEKYLL, ...	A Philanthropist.
MR. HYDE, ...	A Villain.
PRINCE OTTO, ...	Idealists, and late rulers of
PRINCESS SERAPHINA, . .	Grünewald.
KING TEMBINOKA, ...	Of Apemama, South Sea Islands.

SCENE I.—*A moonlight night on Castle Hill, Edinburgh.* ALAN *and* DAVID *are sitting on the wall of the turret which half encloses the great cannon, Mons Meg. Below them lies the city; in the distance the Firth of Forth, and on the horizon the coast of Fife.*

ALAN BRECK: Do ye ken, David, that we're bogles brought back to Auld Reekie by that scribbling warlock, Rab Stevenson?

DAVID BALFOUR: Ay. He's a braw hand at clishmaclaver. I dinna ken why lads and lasses gang aboot reedin' the lees he's writ aboot me and ye, Alan Breck. Ye're no sic a grand maun to be remembered a hundred years syne.

ALAN (*with mock indignation*): Man, I whiles wonder at ye! That was a grand tale he wrote about the fechtin in the roundhouse. Waur I no a bonny

97

fighter, my lad? An' it's a gude thing to have it writ in a book and read by Highlanders the noo. It taks a maun to fecht like that!

DAVID (*rebukingly*): Ye're aye vain of your prowess, Alan. Ye waur a maun the days lang syne, but noo ye're a puir wraith that the sun will drive ben.

ALAN: But Rab Stevenson has gie us life for anither hundred years. And Scots aye talk aboot us when they sit by the ingle-neuk with his bukes i' their loofs.

DAVID: I'm no sayin' he canna write aboot fechtin, and murder, and piratical men, and a' sic wardly things that the Deil inspires. But he's no releegious, Alan; he hae's nae respect for the Auld Kirk; and, therefore, he hae's nae richt to be called a leetary maun.

ALAN: Hoot lad! Ye mak me dour wi' your fashin'. There's Rabbie Burns who writ verses against the Auld Kirk, and did'na we meet him the ither nicht a crackin' jokes amang the ghaists, wi' Sir Walter, and Allan Ramsay, and Dr. John Brown — ay, and his own ne'er-do-weel, Tam o'Shanter, amang them all? It's no the auld Kirk, God bless it alway, but the heart i' a maun that maks him gude. And Rab Stevenson's heart's i' the richt spot.

DAVID (*with his usual caution*): Well, I'm doutsum. There's no enoo' o' the Catechism i' his tales to mak' them leetary. John Knox wouldna approve of them.

98

ALAN (*with indignation*) :   Ye've been a ghaist for a hundred years, livin' abune the clouds, and ye canna see that the Gude Sheperd does'na wait for John Knox to speak before he lets a Scotsman into the leetary fold !

> (*The fog rises from the Firth of Forth, and sweeps up the Castle Hill.   The sun creeps over Arthur's Seat, and as its first ray touches the Castle wall,* ALAN *and* DAVID *vanish in the mist.*)

SCENE II.—*The laboratory of* DR. JEKYLL *in his old London house.   The walls from floor to ceiling are lined with shelves filled with bottles of chemicals.   A table between two windows is covered with retorts, test tubes, etc.   A Bunsen burner is throwing a jet of pale blue flame on a retort filled with a bubbling liquid, in which the globules rise and fall, flashing like many-colored eyes.   A fire is on the hearth, and before it stand* DR. JEKYLL *and* MR. HYDE *in earnest conversation.*

DR. JEKYLL :

THIS writer Stevenson, whose book I hold in my hands, reported me eight years ago as saying, " Man is not truly one, but truly two.   I say two, because the state of my own knowledge does not pass beyond that point.   Others will follow, others will outstrip me on the same lines ; and I hazard the guess that man will be ultimately known for a mere polity of multifarious, incongruous, and independent denizens."   When this was published it was greeted with rapt-

99

ure as the ingenious invention of a clever romancer — a fable to teach a moral truth. But already the guess which I simply hazarded has been scientifically demonstrated by the hypnotic investigations of Charcot, Janet, Binet, and the rest. We now know that by hypnotism a single individual may be divided into three or more personalities, of widely different and often antagonistic traits. Of course no one remembers now that Stevenson, the romancer, was the first to give this truth to the world.

MR. HYDE: You may remember that a good many hundred years before Stevenson or Charcot, there was recorded the case of a man out of whom there were cast *seven* devils.

JEKYLL (*with severity*): We are now talking scientifically. Of course, in literature there have been hints of a dual nature in man—from Adam to Faust. But I do believe that in all his studies of character Stevenson has been more subtile than most modern writers, because he has grasped this idea of the complexity of our motives and actions. He never draws a chalk line between good and bad, but shades the one into the other so gradually that you are in doubt of the relative quality of an action.

HYDE (*with a satirical smile*) : As a man wholly wicked I approve of that. Nothing will so rapidly lead men my way as these vague distinctions.

JEKYLL (*protesting*) : But I am not putting Stevenson forward solely as a moralist ! He is a literary artist who has had the good fortune to grasp a great psychological truth which helps to put his art in line with modern thought.

HYDE (*impatiently*) : Bother modern thought ! Stevenson does not care a rush for it—he is a writer of stories for the sake of the story. Don't load him down with subtilties which never entered his head.

JEKYLL : There was something more than the story in " Prince Otto," " Will o' the Mill," " Olalla," and " The Master of Ballantrae." I'll grant that he would like to be only a teller of entrancing tales, but the blood of the preaching Balfours is too much for him, and he moralizes in spite of himself.

HYDE (*laughing*) : It's pretty bad morality often, I'm glad to say. He has a way of making his wicked men far more attractive than his good ones—which is the way of the world, isn't it, my learned Doctor ?

DR. JEKYLL (*with righteous indignation*) : No, sir ! No ! The motives of our best actions are, I

will admit, always slightly mixed with something base. But in the long run a good action has good motives, and a bad action has bad motives. The world knows that as well as you do, and is attracted or repelled by a man accordingly. If I may be personal, you need only think of the esteem in which I am held in London, and the detestation which follows your every footstep. (*Walks to the table and pours some of the fiery liquid into a glass, which he hands to* HYDE *to drink.*)

HYDE (*jeering as he drinks it*) : And yet *I* am a part of the motive in every philanthropic act of yours ; *I* stand behind your good deeds and say : " You will lose social and scientific caste if you are not respectable." Therefore you *are* respectable ! A fine unmixed motive that is ! (HYDE *springs at* JEKYLL'S *throat. There is a sharp explosion, and a green light fills the room. When it fades out into white,* DR. JEKYLL *is seen alone, sitting in his arm-chair,*

102

with an expression of horror on his face, as though he had just seen and dreaded the return of an awful vision.)

SCENE III.—*The heart of the forest of Grünewald.* PRINCE OTTO *and* PRINCESS SERAPHINA *seated on a fallen tree by the edge of a pool into which a white cascade is plunging.*

PRINCESS SERAPHINA : In this forest we awoke from our dream of Power, and found love; we lost a principality and found each other.

PRINCE OTTO : We fled from ambition and discovered happiness.

SERAPHINA : And now to the world we appear to be only poor refugees—you a hunter and I a housewife—all our glory gone, and nothing to live for !

OTTO : But like Stevenson's '' Lantern-Bearers,'' we carry out of sight, near our hearts, the hidden light which glorifies it all.

SERAPHINA : What an illuminating fable of his that is ! The '' mound of mud '' in which ordinary people seem to dwell is nothing to him ; he is interested only in the golden chamber at the heart of which each dwells delighted.

OTTO : Yes, that is why we always read him with such joy. We know that he will take us on a chase after the '' incommunicable delight of life.''

SERAPHINA : It is what Henry James calls the perpetual boy in him—the glorious zest of living.

OTTO : The song of the nightingale which lured

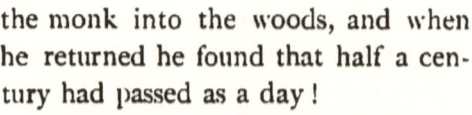

the monk into the woods, and when he returned he found that half a century had passed as a day!

SERAPHINA: I fear Stevenson does not always take us after the nightingale's song. There is a hint of following a bird of prey now and then —a suggestion of carrion which I don't quite like.

OTTO: Oh, but remember that with him it's always on the way to the nightingale's song. If you follow him long enough the path ends in beauty.

SERAPHINA: But he ought to make a detour 'round the carcasses. I should not mind a few briars by the way, but nothing disagreeable. Oh, the awful gore of chapters in "The Wrecker."

OTTO: That is spoken like a woman—it is the physical image of it which repels you. You lose sight of the great passions portrayed in such chapters.

SERAPHINA: He is an avowed disciple of idealism, of romance—a votary of beauty—and he should not spoil his pages, dedicated to beauty, with repellent images. The real joy of life does not lie in that direction. I don't want the smoke and smell of the lantern (to use his own image). I only want to feel its warmth near my heart, and to flash its ray of light into the darkness, now and then.

OTTO: That is always the woman's point of view.

But for the boys on the links (and the men they pre-figure), the pungent odor of the blistering tin of the lantern under their coats is an essential part of that series of sensations which send their imagination soaring away to the Elysian Fields. A man often *must* build his castle in Spain on piles that are driven into the mud.

SERAPHINA: For me the real Stevenson is the author of your story, " Prince Otto," of " Under-woods," " A Child's Garden of Verses," " Virgini-bus," " Will o' the Mill," and " An Inland Voy-age." They are builded so far above the mire.

OTTO: And for me he is the author of " Treasure Island," " Kidnapped," " The Master," " The Wrecker," and " David Balfour." Between the two groups is almost the whole range of the imagination —from the purely idyllic to the most complex passions. He plays upon this wonderful o r g a n, with words for notes— and, oh, the music of them !

SERAPHINA: Y o u get very near the se-cret of his skill as a writer when you say that. It is " the love of lovely words" which leads him on and on,

through " wet woods and miry lane," till at last you can almost hear his song in the water-fall yonder :

> " Where hath fleeting Beauty led ?
> To the doorway of the dead.
> Life is over, life was gay ;
> We have come the primrose way."

EPILOGUE.

THE SONG OF TEMBINOKA, KING OF APEMAMA.

Sing, my warriors, sing ! men of the sharklike race !
Sing of the poet who came and greeted us face to face.
He from the cold, gray North, I, in these tropic isles,
Meet as brothers and bards, with eloquent songs and smiles—

Meet as brothers, though singing words that are strange
and proud—
Pale and wan in his face, while
mine is a thunder-cloud.
But the heart of a man is hidden
by neither language nor
skin—
To love as a man and a brother
maketh the whole world kin.
The tales that he tells are of he-
roes who fought like braves
to the death—
Bone of our bone are these he-
roes, the very breath of our
breath !
Then sing, my warriors, sing !
Men of the sharklike race,
Sing of the poet who came and
greeted us face to face !

106

J. M. BARRIE

"WATTY SCOTT OR JAMIE BARRIE."

THE HOUSEHOLD OF J. M. BARRIE

GAVIN DISHART, ...	{ The little Minister of the Auld Licht Kirk in Thrums.
BABBIE, ...	{ Known as " The Egyptian," married to Gavin.
TAMMAS HAGGART, . .	The Humorist of Thrums.

SCENE : *The summer seat in the garden of the Auld Licht Manse in Thrums. Babbie is seated in the sun of a warmish June day, knitting blue yarn stockings. Enter* GAVIN *from the door of his study, carrying a new book in his hand.*

GAVIN (*sitting near* BABBIE) : He's been at his tricks again.

BABBIE :   Who ?

GAVIN :   Jamie Barrie.   Here's more writin' about us he's been putting in a book.

BABBIE (*looking at him slyly*) :   Does he tell any more tales about a Little Minister who was fooled by an Egyptian ?

GAVIN (*dropping into Scotch, affectionately*) :   Ah, my lassie, but Jamie did mak you braw and bonnie in the buke !   I am

109

no sayin' that you're not a cantie bit stocky wi the licht o' heaven i' your een, but Jamie shudna hae flattered you so to your face.   It's wicked and warldly !

BABBIE (*with a mocking sigh*) : We all have our trials to bear, and it's yours to have a worldly minded woman for a wife.

GAVIN (*indignantly*) : I did not say that, my lass.   I said Jamie Barrie was worldly to put your capers with the soldiers in a book, and to tell everybody that you had a bonnie face.

BABBIE (*roguishly*) :   Well, haven't I ?

GAVIN (*cannily*) :   Some might think so.   I have no definite opinion.

BABBIE (*with flashing eyes*) :   You haven't, my little minister ?   Then what did you mean by your compliments that evening when you came to meet me at Nanny Webster's well ?   I'll have you up before Tammas Whamond and the session of the kirk for deceit and false speaking.

GAVIN (*laughing*) :   Oh, but I love to rouse the Egyptian in your flashing black eyes !   They glow with fire like Loch Lomond at sunset.

BABBIE (*demurely*) :   And you, an Auld Licht minister, blethering like that to a woman who has been your wife for a year !   You're what Tammas Haggart calls a " blaw-i'-my-lug."

GAVIN (*who has learned her ways*) : A man, even a minister, soon learns to manage his wife by telling her what she likes to hear. Tammas gave me that advice soon after I married you, and he is a wise man.

BABBIE : Tammas has been spoiled because Jamie Barrie put him in his book. The other day he spoke to me about "me and Rab Burns and other leetary men." He was finding fault with your sermon at the time as hardly up to his standard.

GAVIN : Barrie may have spoiled Tammas a little, but Thrums, as a whole, is proud of his books. I think I understand my people better by reason of them.

BABBIE (*seriously*) : Yes, he has put in his books the heroism of poverty. It is so easy to put a rich and titled hero in a book, but to show heroism in narrow and forbidding circumstances, like Jess and Hendry's, in "A Window in Thrums," is a very difficult thing.

GAVIN : He does more than that. He shows you the compensations of poverty. All the books I used to study at the University made poverty a hateful thing—a blot on the fair earth. But Barrie's Thrums' weavers teach a different lesson.

BABBIE : And we who live among them know how much better off they are than many of the rich. I know I should be happier in Jess's cottage than I was in Lord Rintoul's castle.

"IT IS SO EASY TO PUT A RICH AND TITLED HERO IN A BOOK."

III

GAVIN (*putting on his severe preacher's manner*): It's the fear of the Lord that glorifies the life of rich and poor alike.

BABBIE (*mischievously*): I am not so sure of that. It's only the poor who fear the Lord; the rich patronize Him. I know, for I've lived with both kinds.

"THE RICH PATRONIZE HIM."

GAVIN (*a little shocked*): We must not jest with serious things.

BABBIE (*confidently*): There is nothing wrong in telling the truth. Barrie sees it clearer than we do here. It is absolute fidelity to their affections that makes people worth anything, whether they be rich or poor. That is why the great world has laughed and cried over the "Window in Thrums." They looked right into the heart of that little family and found everything clean, and genuine, and honest.

GAVIN (*admiringly*): What a little philosopher I have married! And I thought she was only a half-wild Egyptian!

BABBIE: Oh, I'll be writing your sermons yet, and the session will wake up to listen.

GAVIN: You can

"THE GREAT WORLD HAS LAUGHED AND CRIED OVER 'THE WINDOW IN THRUMS.'"

begin by telling me what to say at the Literary Club which meets to-night at the Town House. Haggart asked me yesterday to take part in the discussion. He came into my study with unusual solemnity, and said that after prayerful consideration the Club had decided that the time had arrived to discuss the question whether Watty Scott or Jamie Barrie was the greatest Scottish novelist. Dite Walls is to read a poem on the subject, and Mr. Dickie is to compare Scott and Homer.

"HE CAME INTO MY STUDY WITH UNUSUAL SOLEMNITY."

BABBIE: Evidently Mr. Dickie does not put Barrie in the same class with Scott and Homer?

GAVIN: Oh, no. You know he is the free-thinking schoolmaster from Tilliedrum, and is a little jealous of the recent literary eminence of Thrums. The other day he said to me, contemptuously: " Jamie Barrie is nought but a U. P. minister turned to writin' tales, and ower poor tales at that. Watty Scott wudna ever hae thocht that Tammas Haggart was sarceestic."

BABBIE (*smiling*): What does Tammas himself think of Barrie?

GAVIN: Here he is, coming for my answer about attending the Club. Let us ask him.

(Enter TAMMAS HAGGART.*)*

HAGGART *(bowing)* :   Hoo's a' wi ye?   And are ye coomin' the nicht to the Leetary Club?

GAVIN :   Ay, and I am hoping to hear your views about Jamie.

BABBIE :   As I can't be there to hear, won't you tell me what you're going to say, Tammas?

HAGGART *(in deep thought)* :   I dinna ken yet. As I hae often said to Jamie Barrie, "Humour spouts oot by itsel." It will be humourous, nae doot, and Davit Lunan winna be able to see the place to lauch. Davit is daft.

BABBIE :   But you'll praise Jamie's books, won't you? We can't let Mr. Dickie go back to Tillie-drum and say we're ashamed of our ain bairn.

HAGGART :   He'll no do that. I mean to be sae sarceestic to Mr. Dickie, that he'll go ben to Tillie-drum wi' respect for all of us.

BABBIE *(impatiently)* :   But what do you think of Mr. Barrie?

HAGGART *(meditatively)* :   Jamie is no a humourist like mysel. Jamie is what, i' the minister's presence, I may call a Romanticalicist, and when I say that, I ken that Waster Lunny will think he knows what I am haverin' aboot. But naebody, even the minister, kens what I mean by a Romanticalicist. *(Laughing to himself.)* Ay, maun, but that's a fine bit o' sarcasm. *(Rubbing his chin.)* What I mean by it is that Jamie Barrie sees the outside of hoo we all live in Thrums,

114

but he doesna grasp the real inards of it. So he maks up the inards oot of his ain head and writes it on paper, and calls it a true tale. We are no sae glaikit as he maks us. We were no born on the Sawbath.

GAVIN: But he does not say we are glaikit (silly).

HAGGART (*irritated*): He put it doon in writin' that Tammas Haggart said, " A body canna be expeckit baith to mak the joke an to see't ; that would be doin' twa fowk's wark." I ken better than that. I've made a joke and seen't mysel at the same time— but no vera often. I *always* see the joke within a week o' makin' it.

BABBIE: I know you do, and I'll tell Jamie so the next time he comes to Thrums.

(MARGARET *calls from the door that Wearywarld has come to see the minister. All exeunt.*)

"IVE MADE A JOKE AND SEEN IT MYSEL AT THE SAME TIME."

THE HOME OF ROMANCE

THE HOME OF ROMANCE

THE WISE ADRIAN, ... } of New York, and recently
THE GENTLE DIANA, . . . } wedded.

SCENE: *The deck of a steamer on the Caledonian Canal, between Banavie and Inverness, in the Highlands of Scotland.*

TIME: *The Present—midsummer.*

ADRIAN: They like to call this the " Home of Romance," as though the Scottish landscape were responsible for it all. The true home of romance is the warm heart of a man or woman—and you can easily find that in other lands than the Highlands.

DIANA: Even in New York? ·

ADRIAN: I found it there—but what a search I made for it! I began to think that it was as elusive as the Philosopher's stone. One day, when I was despairing, I met *you*.

DIANA: But I don't turn what I touch into gold.

ADRIAN: Oh, no. I've already found out that you reverse the process. You turn gold into anything that takes your fancy. We have ten trunks

119

filled with the results of your necromancy. Think of the duty on them !

DIANA : Yes—a real home of romance comes high. But you should be thankful that I am a simple villa, and not a great castle with scores of retainers. They *are* expensive.

ADRIAN : You shall always be "just as high as my heart."

DIANA : I'll remind you of that some day. It isn't safe to make pretty speeches to a tyrannical wife.

ADRIAN : Very well—we'll have lots of old scores to settle up "some day." I'm making note of them, because you know we *can't* disagree on our wedding journey.

DIANA : I can. For instance, I think you are all wrong in poking fun at the Scotch for calling this the "home of romance." Think of the romantic places we have seen in the past three days. (*Rapidly turns the leaves of a guide-book.*) There was the place where *Roderick Dhu* and *Fitz-James* fought in the Trossachs.

ADRIAN : A quiet little bit of forest, that no one would look at if Sir Walter had not written a poem.

DIANA : And there was *Ellen's Isle*.

ADRIAN : Sir Walter again—you would never have mentioned it if he had not.

DIANA (*impatiently*) : But think of Oban, and Dunstaffnage Castle, and the Cataract of Connel— all in an hour.

ADRIAN: Yes; William Black, Professor Blackie, and Ossian are responsible for your interest in them. I also have read the guide-book.

DIANA: Ugh! You are a horrid, horrid—what you call it—*iconoclast*. But you can't say anything mean about Ben Nevis. Think what a view we had of him this morning. Did you ever see a finer mingling of grays and greens and browns, with patches of purple, when the sun came out? And over it all the blue-white mist crowning his stately head.

ADRIAN: Yes, all that, and noted besides for (*quoting*) " the distillery from which comes the celebrated whiskey called ' Long John ' or ' Dew of Ben Nevis ' " That is what makes it dear to the heart of the Scot.

DIANA (*desperately*): But wasn't " The Well of Heads " awe-inspiring—terrible?

ADRIAN: A nice old rock with seven heads very badly carved on it, and an inscription commemorating a very bloody ending to an old feud, which simply isn't in for gore with the McCoy-Hatfield feud in our own country. You would not travel very far at home to see the tomb of all the McCoys, would you?

DIANA: But I would to see such a sight as the " Falls of Foyers " where we climbed at the last landing.

ADRIAN: Simply because Burns wrote

" Among the heathy hills and ragged woods
The roaring Foyers pours his mossy floods."

Now Bryant wrote better poetry than that about the Kaaterskill Falls at home, and yet you made fun of them last summer " because they turn them on for a quarter apiece."

DIANA (*laughing*) : It was funny, wasn't it ?— and the excuse is that the money goes to the Methodists. It ought to be Baptist money.

ADRIAN : But honestly, Diana, Scotland is the home of romance because it is the home of Scott, Burns, Black, Macdonald, Stevenson, and Barrie— and of thousands of men, like that old Highlander in kilts on the tow-path, who loves what they have written. I would wager he has a copy of Burns in his sporran, and has quoted him a half dozen times to the grim Celt who is walking with him. Those old boys don't read for excitement or for knowledge, but because they love their land, and their people, and their religion—and their great writers simply express for them those emotions in words they can understand. You and I come over here with thousands of our countrymen, to *borrow* their emotions. It *is* lovely, it *is* romantic, and it stirs your heart and mine, because we were raised on Scott and Burns. In England we travel from place to place in the same way on a wave of memory and emotion, because we have always read the great Englishmen who loved their country and honored it by writing about it with feeling.

DIANA : It is almost as bad as loving another man's wife and neglecting your own.

ADRIAN : And yet these Britishers accuse us of bragging about our country ! The millionaire from Oshkosh may—but our writers don't. Many of them hardly show it decent respect.

DIANA : The old school did — Hawthorne, Cooper, Simms, Brockden Brown, Emerson, Whittier.

ADRIAN : And their works endure in the hearts of their countrymen. But the men of to-day—aren't they building up a beautiful set of literary associations for their countrymen ? Imagine our descendants making pilgrimages to the house where our *Daisy Millers* were (according to tradition) supposed to have lived and spoken bad English ; where our *Tom Sawyers* locked in their school teachers ; to the ruins of the Tuxedo Club to see where *Charley Rich* broke his stick and swore horribly when he was refused by *Miss Million ;* to Beacon Street in search of the lamp-post under which *Miss Prudence* stood wher she consulted with her Soul !

DIANA : That's enough. I know the whole tribe, and I would not walk half a block if I were assured that I could shake hands with any one of them in the flesh. But see, there is the sun shining on the Castle of Inverness, and the purple hills, and a gleam of Moray Firth ! It is lovely and I love it, and it is the end of a beautiful day.

ADRIAN : Then why do you look pensive?

DIANA (*laughing*) : I was thinking by contrast of the way in which the sinking sun strikes the red tower of the Produce Exchange, and old Liberty's halo, and the Brooklyn Elevators——

ADRIAN: And the Multifloor Apartment House on Fifty-ninth Street, and a six-room flat.

DIANA: Yes—home.

ADRIAN: The Home of our Romance.

(*Chorus of 'bus drivers:* " *Royal Hotel, sir,*" " *Culloden Inn,*" " *Sutherland Arms,*" " *Take you right up.*")

A LITTLE DINNER IN ARCADY

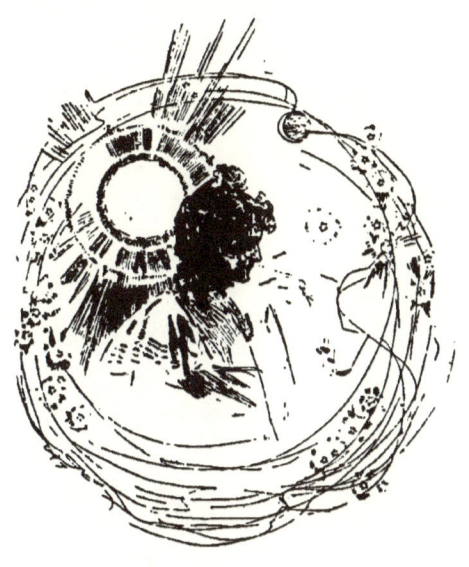

A LITTLE DINNER IN ARCADY.*

LIFE and MISS FANNY DE SIÈCLE (costume after Gibson).

MR. HOWELLS and MISS DIANA (of The Crossways).

MR. JAMES and THE EGYPTIAN (of Thrums).

MR. CRAWFORD and MISS DAISY MILLER (of Schenectady, N. Y.).

MR. BUNNER and MRS. HAUKSBEE (of Simla).

MR. PAGE and PRINCESS SARACINESCA (of Rome).

MR. MEREDITH and MEH LADY (of Virginia).

MR. KIPLING and MISS PENELOPE LAPHAM (of Boston).

MR. BARRIE and MISS MIDGE (of South Washington Square).

SCENE.—*A round table in the Octagon room of a wayside inn, over-looking the Valley of Arcady. In the centre of the table, a mound of flowers, on which appears the motto, " While there's Life there's Hope." The ladies of the party wear costumes which represent many different styles of the past decade, and are evidently suspicious of the social standing of each other. The men have long known each other in Arcady, are more at ease, but are evidently not quite sure that they approve of the ladies. As the dinner advances and the wine-glasses are filled and refilled with Falernian and Nectar, the constraint vanishes and everybody talks.*

M ISS FAN (*to* LIFE, *who is in love with her*) : You dear boy, why *did* you give me the place of honor at the table ?

* Written for the Jubilee Number of *Life.*

LIFE : Because you are the bud of the past decade, and you will be the perfect flower of the coming one. Every man of us here would rather please you than all the rest of the world.

MISS FAN : What a dance I lead you! Don't you find that I am hard to please?

LIFE (*with intention*) : You are always kind to me, dear.

MISS FAN : For that pretty speech I'll try to be gracious. But honestly, boy, I don't like your guests—the women I mean. They are hardly in our set. Where did you pick them up?

LIFE : I told each man to bring one of his own family. Then I mixed the names in a hat and drew this combination.

MISS FAN : Well, I hope they like it, but I'm sure Mr. Howells looks bored.

LIFE : Why, Diana is the brightest woman at the table, but very romantic. See the " flashing arrows in her eyes" while she talks !

DIANA (*to* LIFE) : I know you are talking about me—but I'll forgive you if it was kind. I've been telling Mr. Howells that I like his American girls, but not his married women—they are so censorious.

HOWELLS : They don't call it that hard name in Boston ; it is simply " accumulating materials for a correct diagnosis of character."

MISS LAPHAM : We are not *all* given to backbiting in Boston. Most of us are charitable.

MISS FAN (*aside to* HOWELLS): She is not quite in the swim in Boston, is she? Old Silas Lapham's daughter? (*raising her eyebrows*) Paint?

MEH LADY: You Northern gyurls shouldn't be so critical of folks. We all simply flatter our sweethearts, and lead them 'round with a gold chain.

DAISY MILLER: Well, I like that! Think of our flattering Charley Rich and his set. They are so conceited now that they think all the girls are in love with them. We have to train all the young nobs down with sarcasm before they are endurable. We are onto their style.

PRINCESS SARACINESCA (*to* PAGE): What queer English that young woman speaks! I fear that I must have had an uncultivated teacher in Rome. It's all so strange to me.

PAGE: You must come and visit us in Ole Vahginia, my deah lady, to heah the real old English language. We are descended from the Cavaliers, madam.

PRINCESS: Now, I understand the peculiar spelling in "Marse Chan." It's old English, isn't it, like Chaucer and Beowulf?

PAGE (*shifting the subject*): Oh, I say, Meh Lady, you must invite the Princess down to the old plantation. She is writing a book about America, and I reckon it will be all

129

FAN.

Boston and New York as usual, unless we divert her.

MRS. HAUKSBEE: Invite me too, please. I want to see America. I only know what I've read about it in Mr. James's novels, and what Mr. Kipling has told me.

BUNNER (*behind his hand to* PAGE): She must have a beautiful chromo picture of us then in her mental gallery. Imagine taking your impression of America from James and Kipling!

KIPLING (*laughing*): Come, now, Bunner, I could not help hearing. Have not I atoned for the sins of my youth with "The Naulahka?" Isn't *Tarvin* a good American?

BUNNER: He's not a real American; only a newspaper American, made by the drummer and the "funny man."

KIPLING: And never met with outside of *Puck!*

BARRIE: What I've come over here to see is a real American girl.

MISS FAN (*with a glance around the table*): You won't find her in contemporary novels.

DAISY MILLER (*consciously*): I think Mr. James has done us justice.

MISS FAN (*maliciously*): Oh, yes, he has done justice to some of the freaks we annually export.

JAMES (*calmly*): Why do you keep some of your best freaks at home then? I can't make bricks without straw.

MEH LADY (*gently*): We are not all nervous and
130

impertinent over here.   Come, visit us oftener, Mr. James.

THE MIDGE: Oh, who would say so cruel a thing about us?   I've found everybody so kind in New York.

MISS FAN (*aside to* LIFE):   A little Bohemian from the French quarter—that kind is always generous.   They live in such a little bit of a world and have to help each other.

THE EGYPTIAN: It seems to me that all you American girls know too much.   You have no illusions, no romance.   In Scotland we still occasionally die for the man we love.

MISS FAN: How horrid!   Over here that sort of thing only happens in Bowery hotels, among foreigners.

BARRIE: Ay.   But what does the real American lass do for the man she loves with all her soul?

MISS FAN: Marries him, every time.   He can't escape her, and would not if he could.   That is why I don't approve of you good people who write our novels.   You make us so shallow in our artifices, and often so vulgar and impertinent.   Really, don't you see that the girl of the period uses *finesse* with sincerity?   That is where you misinterpret us.   We are not artificial; we simply combine the business tact that we inherit from our fathers, with the fidelity and religious instincts that we inherit from our mothers.

KIPLING: A sort of combination of the best traits of *Becky Sharp* and *Amelia Sedley*—

CRAWFORD : With a considerable addition of jewelry and frocks. It seems to me that you more than ever overdress the part of the ingénue.

MISS FAN : Another of the mistakes of our novelists ! Our beautiful frocks have raised the art standards of the country. Our fathers have been forced to build houses and buy furniture, and fixtures, and broughams to accord with the lovely costumes of their charming daughters. A fine jewel must have an appropriate setting, and we've got it.

HOWELLS : Very well, how would you have us picture the girl of the new decade, Miss Fan ?

MISS FAN : She must be, like my dear Diana, " A man and woman for brains ; " her beauty will be the flower of health ; her wit, the polish of the world ; her sympathy, the result of a true insight into our " moral predicament," as Mr. James delights to call it. She will be a patriot and an optimist always.

MEREDITH : I like to hear you say that. I am getting to be an old man, but I believe more and more in the promptings of nature in youth. How can any one live near to nature without being an optimist ! I don't mean the trees and flowers only— but near to men and women who live and suffer, and hope.

HOWELLS (*rising*) : Here's to the flower of the century—the American Girl ! May we love her in our homes, do her full justice in our books, and wear her image in our hearts !

MISS FAN : And here's to the eyes of the next

century, through which posterity will see us—the American Novelist! May he always picture us as good as we are, and *never* better than we ought to be!

LIFE: And here's confusion to all Critics who refuse to appreciate the American Girl and the American Novelist!

THE END.

www.ingramcontent.com/pod-product-compliance
Lightning Source LLC
Chambersburg PA
CBHW020405030726
47496CB00007B/2317